First Edition Jan 2020
Second Edition June 2023

ISBN 978-1-7350329-9-3 (ppr)
ISBN 978 -1-7350329-5-6 (ebk)
ISBN 978-1-7350329-0-0 (hdbk)

*This book is for you, God; I'm thankful for the dreams and nightmares that inspired this story.*

**Disclaimer/Warnings:**

This series and stories contained within are a work of fiction. Names, characters, businesses, places, events, locales, and other details are products of the author's imagination. Any resemblance to actual persons, living or dead, or actual events is purely coincidental. This story is intended for an adult audience. This series and stories contained within may contain descriptions of events that may be identified as triggers for certain readers. These stories may contain details of abuse, alcohol use, death, mental health, rape, sexual abuse, violence, and war. This is not a full list of possible triggers.

Please proceed at your own risk.

# IN SHADOWS LIE

T. Emiller

Cover Art By: Ed Espitia

# Contents

# Chapter 1

## *Have you seen my dog?*

Beams of light from the setting sun danced through radiant blooms that clung to the boughs of countless trees. In the distance, the joyful air filtered through a large open doorway, across the back of a woman's neck. Liana lifted her head from the sizable desk in the corner of her room as locks of her pale blonde hair fell, and covered her sapphire blue eyes. The computer screen in front of her glared back menacingly. She heaved a sigh when she saw that the number of emails from her work inbox had tripled since she last attempted to tackle them.

Her tangled tresses fell past her shoulders as she pushed them out of her face. With a yawn, she leaned back in her chair and stretched her arms behind her head. She glanced over at the massive pile of coarse black fur that made up her companion, Striker. His ears perked up at the sudden attention, yet he didn't bother to lift his head. With a short laugh, Liana got to her feet and crossed the spacious room. The dark cherry wood floor led her to an open hallway accented with vaulted ceilings.

"Maybe a snack will spark some motivation," she said to Striker, who grumbled from a distance.

She opened the door to the fridge, leaned in, and looked around for something of interest. As the cold air of the fridge rushed past her, she tugged at her oversized, emerald sweatshirt. Liana grabbed a bottle of chocolate milk, opened it, and sniffed it slightly. After a short shrug, she took a drink. She was filled with instant regret when she realized it was the wrong choice.

She almost tripped over her own feet as she ran for the sink and coughed up the milk. She rinsed her mouth quickly in the faucet before dumping the rest of the milk down the drain. After she tossed the container in a bin, she headed back down the hallway toward her bedroom. Liana no longer felt the need for any snack. Striker let out a soft whimper and appeared behind her.

"Yea, yea," she said.

Liana moved past her light oak four-poster bed with sheer navy drapes that coiled around the posts, to the glass sliding door at the back of the room. She looked back for Striker, who pranced up the hall with his leash.

He lifted his head slightly to nudge her in the stomach. A dramatic eye roll crossed her face as she fastened the new leash to Striker's leather collar. As he walked out of the door to the densely wooded, unfenced yard of hers, she let the strap fall to the ground behind him.

The cold stone radiated through her socks to her feet as she stepped out onto the patio. Her hands found her hips while she took a deep breath of the fresh spring air. Liana looked to her right, at the house where she expected her neighbor to be fast asleep. Karen was a bitter, aged woman who lived with her husband and had a bit of extra time on her hands. She loved to speak to Liana about anything, and everything and Liana didn't have the heart to cut her off.

The latest topic was Liana's "pest" of a dog. Of course, it went unnoticed how well-mannered Liana's "horse" was, only his size and slobber were on the agenda. All she ever had to say was how he needed restrained and how Liana should be careful that he doesn't attack anyone.

Liana grinned from the small taste of victory as she looked out at Striker, who frolicked through the bushes like a pup.

*He is,* she thought to herself, *technically on a leash.*

Liana sat down on a small iron bench near the glass doors. The peaceful sounds of crickets chirped all around as lightning bugs danced through the trees and accented the evening with a charming glow. As she leaned back on the bench, she gazed up at the stars and began to lose herself in thought. Liana loved being able to look up and see the stars, to pretend she was someone else, somewhere else. One of the many perks of living further away from the city where the stars were so easily visible. Though she couldn't convince any of her friends to do the same, she was okay with that.

As a chill crept in the air, she pulled her knees to her chest and tucked them under her sweatshirt. She started to wonder how long it was going to take before Striker was ready to come inside. With a shiver, she got to her feet to go back inside, and thought she'd just leave the door open for him to come in when he was ready. As she turned to head to the bedroom, she glanced around the yard and realized she didn't see him at all anymore. When she turned back toward the trees and saw nothing, she squinted into the darkness and gave a short whistle. After she waited a moment and heard nothing in response, she stepped to the edge of the stone patio.

"Striker," she called out, with only silence in return.

Liana bent slightly, pulled her socks from her feet, and threw them behind her onto her bedroom floor. The grass was damp and springy between her toes as she stepped onto it. A cool breeze blew in her hair while she walked into the trees. The further she went, the more her pace slowed. There was an eerie stillness in the air, and the last of the day's light seemed to have been swallowed up in the tops of the trees as she was barely able to see much around her.

After she walked through a few rows of trees, she stumbled on a small clearing. A pond lay before her, with a tiny stream that dribbled over rocks and pebbles, accompanied by minuscule dots of color from wildflowers beginning to bloom. A dense fog rose from the water and gradually moved across the banks. The cool, silky, blanket crept up to meet Liana's toes.

Liana turned back toward her home and wondered how far she had gone. Nothing looked familiar anymore. She never ventured this far into the forest for fear of getting consumed in it. As she turned, something caught her by the wrist. When she tugged against it and still met resistance, she turned to look at what was impeding her return.

A look of bewilderment consumed her when she realized her wrist was in the grip of someone's hand. Her gaze followed the clutch of the hand up to its owner. Quickly, she pulled against him and stared at him, confused and slightly alarmed. He towered over her in height, with shoulder-length light blonde, messy hair that was accented by a trim beard.

*Who is this guy?* Liana thought to herself, *What is he doing out here?*

He wasn't saying anything, yet he didn't release her. A shadow cast over his face, making it barely visible in the fading light.

She spoke quietly, almost in a whisper, "Let go... What are you doing out here? Have you… seen a do-"

He put a finger to her lips and silenced her as he looked off behind her. His skin smelled of pine and cedar and was hot to the touch. She backed away from his hand and looked at him questioningly as she pulled at her arm again. Suddenly his demeanor changed, and she could tell something was wrong. Seizing the moment, she yanked her arm away from him, and freed herself from his grasp, yet her eyes stayed locked on him. Fear riddled his face as his focus darted behind her.

"Run!" he yelled suddenly, in a deep voice.

She jumped in response to his sudden outburst yet remained where she stood. Paralyzed, she stared on in complete confusion.

His eyes locked with hers and he insisted more urgently, "They're coming for you! Just run!"

Liana woke with a fright, clinging to her tangled mess of blankets as she fell partially out of her bed, face just above the floor. The darkness of her room seemed to fade, and she was left gasping for air. Startled half to death, she pulled herself the rest of the way onto her bed. Slow, deep breaths filled Liana's lungs as she sat for a moment and replayed the dream in her mind a thousand times.

"Only a dream…" she whispered to herself as her eyes darted around the room, concerned about the truth in her statement, "a dream."

Moments passed before she shook it off. It didn't seem as disturbing as she thought about the events that took place, but she couldn't shake the sensation of fear. Nightmares were something she grew accustomed to after years of feeling trapped in them, but this one felt so real.

Liana tugged the comforter off and kicked it to the floor. She untangled herself from the sheets and hopped out of bed. As she made contact with the floor, she slipped. Her hand caught one of the bedposts, and saved her from a painful meeting with the ground. Out of the corner of her eye, she caught sight of the object that had caught her off guard as it slid across the wood. It was merely a sock.

*Wait a sec,* she thought to herself.

She looked at her feet, bare and grass-stained, then up at the sliding glass door that stood open. She slowly walked to the back door, placed her hands on the framing, leaned out, and looked around.

"Striker," she whispered tentatively. With a look to the right, she leaned out a little more, then looked to the left. "Striker," she whispered again.

The shock of a cold, wet nose on her leg caused her to let out a tiny squeal. A sigh of relief escaped her as she saw that her canine companion sat behind her. She slowly closed the sliding glass door and gave Striker a pat on the head. Liana decided to get an early start on her day since she was a little too on edge to get back to sleep.

At the granite island in the center of her kitchen, Liana ate breakfast as the news blared in the front room. Though she stared straight at the television, the words of the news anchor slipped by her. The feelings of the dream still weighed on her and she couldn't help but feel drawn to the man somehow. She wondered what he was talking about.

*It was just,* she thought to herself while she shook her head, *a dream.*

After a quick change of clothes, Liana grabbed a duffel bag from the foyer. She shut the door behind her and walked down the stones that led to the circular driveway in front of her home. When she opened the door of her charcoal gray SUV, she tossed in her bag. As the vehicle growled to life, she moved quickly to turn the volume of the music down. After all, it was a bit loud for the morning Liana.

○ ○ ○

Her arrival at the gym, to an extremely bare parking lot was just the way she liked it, and lifted her spirits. As she entered the main hall, a buff receptionist greeted her with an enthusiastic smile. His tightly buzzed hair matched his sharp facial features that were accented by his bright cobalt eyes.

"Just couldn't stay away?" he asked in a smug tone as he walked out from behind the desk toward her.

"Op, you caught me," she said while she pointed at him, sarcasm thick in her voice.

Liana stayed for a moment and admired the man's white polo shirt; it contrasted well with his dark skin and was snug in all the right places. Small talk wasn't on her list of strengths, and it was much too early for her to try to force it. Several times she attempted to duck by him, but he insisted on talking with her. While she attempted to be polite, she nodded and smiled, but she couldn't focus on whatever he was trying to say.

"Anyway," he said as he playfully smacked her arm and tuned her back to the conversation, "If you ever need a personal trainer."

He winked at her and walked back to greet someone else as they walked through the door. She sighed, relieved, and made her way to the locker room. She paused for only a moment to drop her bag before she headed through another door to a long hallway. To save herself the exhaustion of avoiding people, she made her way to the ladies' only section of the fitness center.

Thankfully the room was empty. Mind-numbing electronic music blared from her earbuds as she made her rounds on the various machines. Before long, she decided to hit the pool for a couple of laps. As she made her way out of the equipment room, she smiled awkwardly to the only other woman in the room, who ran vigorously on a treadmill.

The water helped her relax, and after only a few laps, she felt restored. Finally, she was able to shake the feeling of dread that the night's sleep had brought. After a few extra laps, she decided to shower and have a couple of laughs with the guys at the front desk before she headed to work.

# Chapter 2

## *Bosses Orders*

The sun was fully shining when Liana arrived at Stotlie Capel Gaming Enterprises' headquarters. The drive to the large campus was a long two hours into the city from the smaller suburbs where Liana lived, but she didn't mind the commute.

SCGE was the world's leading video game developer. Liana worked in one of the many buildings on the enormous campus that made up the corporation's lead developing institute. She spent her days managing a team of individuals as they developed, tested, and fixed video games before they released them to the public.

Liana parked in the back of the large empty parking garage. Most of her coworkers didn't show up until later in the afternoon, but she arrived early, as usual. After all, it was nearly impossible for her to get anything done with the lively team her boss gave her for the current project.

The lobby of the corporation's central office greeted Liana with a sizeable fountain that lay at the center of a blue and silver mosaic floor. As she made her way into the building, she nodded good morning to the security guard positioned behind a long silver desk behind the fountain. To the right of the guard stood an unadorned silver door with no handle. Liana scanned her badge and pressed the door open before she made her way down a hall of elevators.

She approached the last elevator and scanned her badge over the sensor. Once it arrived, Liana entered and swiped her badge again before she pressed the button for the 7th floor. As the doors closed, she took a step back, shifted to the side, and leaned her shoulder against the cold wall.

"Well, good morning," a voice sounded from behind her.

Liana jumped and glanced over her shoulder at the man from which the voice had come. He was a lean individual with thick, jet-black hair. It fell in a messy state just over his dark eyebrows, accenting his high cheekbones and carved chin. Intrusive eyes of a deep brown, almost black, studied Liana as a smug grin spread across his face. He may have intrigued her, had she not almost wet herself. She gained her composure and nodded with a half-smile in his direction.

"Good morning," she murmured, almost a whisper as her voice evaded her.

The elevator seemed to take an eternity to reach its destination. Eventually, the doors opened, and Liana stepped out into a small lobby with windows to the left and right that overlooked the campus. Frosty panes of glass acted as walls opposite of the elevator. A cheerful redhead with chin-length wavy hair, bright green eyes, and distinctive freckles, sat behind a waist-high, blue and silver desk, the front of which read *Team Alpha Designing*.

"Morning Jessica," Liana said when she regained her voice and smiled at the ambitious younger woman.

"Lia! Hey! We missed you last night. You should've stuck around," Jessica retorted exuberantly while she leaned on her elbows over the desk.

They had quickly become friends after Liana saved her from the wrath of their boss. He was close to firing Jessica after she had mistakenly canceled a critical appointment of his.

"Aw…yea, sorry. Next time for sure," Liana assured.

Liana wasn't much for hanging out. She had gone out once with Jessica a couple of weeks ago and always got invited to things since then. Though she had a decent time, Liana preferred quiet nights in instead.

"Hold you to it!" Jessica squealed.

Jessica gave a thumbs-up before she turned to attend to the man who had startled Liana in the elevator. He now wore a puzzled look on his face as he glanced about the lobby.

*Awesome,* Liana thought to herself as she moved past the desk to the right where another silver door stood.

She scanned her badge to gain access to it and pushed open the door which immediately knocked into someone.

"Oh, goodness! Sorry!" she exclaimed.

Liana cringed as she saw she had knocked into her boss's short, stocky frame. He had, in turn, knocked into the person he walked with. She hadn't seen who the other individual was, only their back was visible. Liana did notice the stranger was holding a cup of coffee or at least a cup that previously held coffee before her boss had knocked into them.

"Liana," her boss exclaimed, more excited than displeased, "just who I was looking for!"

His rosy, plump cheeks pulled into a broad grin and caused his eyes to squint almost to the point where they closed.

A sarcastic tone set in as she started to respond, "Well isn't that ju-"

"Liana, I want you to meet Nicolai," he interrupted and gestured to the coffee stained individual to his left.

"Oh, I'm so sorry Ni-"

She extended her hand to greet him, but as he turned, she froze mid-sentence. His eyes, a deep blue, locked on hers and held her in an oddly familiar grasp.

"Nicolai… Nic is fine though," he said with a deep voice. He took her hand in his and gave her a firm handshake.

"Right, Nic. Sorry," she said with a cringe while she gestured to his shirt and continued to stare at him, while she tried to figure out where she'd seen him before.

"Anyway, Liana, Nicolai is here as your organizational assistant." Her boss rambled on about Nicolai's impressive background, all of which Liana cared nothing about.

*What the heck,* she thought to herself, *is an organizational assistant?*

Not paying a world of attention to her boss, her gaze remained fixated on Nicolai as she wondered if she knew him from somewhere previously.

"He'll be helping you along with- Oh, hey!" her boss exclaimed and looked past her. "Casimir!"

He extended a hand around Liana as she broke her gaze and turned to see who was behind her. Her stare landed on none other than the guy from the elevator.

"Just in time. Casimir, this is Liana. Liana, Casimir," Mr. Kohaim shot back and forth with excitement.

"Casimir was it?" she said with a fake exuberance in her voice and attempted to mock her boss's energy; though it didn't seem to faze him.

Casimir caught Liana's tone and let out a brief chuckle. With a smile, he addressed her, "Sure is."

His presence was gravitational, with a laugh and smile that pulled her in like a force she'd never felt before.

"Liana," her boss spoke again, and immediately snapped her out of the stupor that Casimir's presence had invoked. "Casimir and Nicolai will be your assistants to assure that quality games are making it to the public in record time!"

He grinned at her ecstatically as if this was the news to make her day.

"Show 'em around and help 'em settle in, won't ya? Let's beat those deadlines!" His final harsh words were accented by a few choice finger points at Liana before he turned and shuffled off to his office at the back of the large open room of cubicles.

"Yes, of course!" she said to his back as he walked away, then gradually turned to the two men who stood beside her. "Again, sorry about the shirt," she muttered, and gestured to Nicolai's pressed white shirt that was now coffee stained.

Liana turned and walked along a row of empty cubicles. Casimir smirked at Nicolai, then followed close behind Liana, and asked endless questions. She made her way to the center of the large, open office space, where a high walled, spacious cubicle stood.

"Dress is casual by the way, except for the first Thursday of each month. The corporate managers tour our offices, and Mr. Kohaim likes us to look professional."

She turned to the two men that followed her and caught sight of two cubicles across the aisle from hers. The nameplates on the cubicles read Nicolai Fortescue and Casimir Eles. Liana loved it when Jessica was on her A-game.

"Guess these are yours. I'll give you a moment to get settled in," she said while she motioned to the desks.

Liana turned to her cubicle and saw there were two welcome packets at her desk. She grabbed the packets and slowly sat in her tall chair while she flipped through them to ensure the information was thorough enough and up to date. With everything looking in order, she turned and hopped down from her chair simultaneously. Her timing couldn't have been worse as her face met the chest of Casimir. She let out a small grunt, half with surprise and half with knocking into the solid man and stepped back as the papers scattered across the floor.

"I'm so sorry. Here, let me help you with those," Casimir said as he stooped to help Liana gather the contents of the folders.

He was close enough that his cologne wafted to her. She didn't know what it was, but he smelled wonderful and couldn't help but stare up at him while she fumbled with the papers. At his current position, his hair was long enough to cover his eyes, so she figured he wouldn't notice her stares.

After a moment, she caught sight of Nic behind him, who stared right at her. She quickly looked down at her papers again, and hoped Nicolai didn't take much notice.

"Here you go," Casimir said as they stood, and he handed her some of the documents he had gathered.

"These were actually for you and uh..." she trailed off as she looked down; disheartened at the stack of papers that were now shuffled together.

"Nicolai," Casimir said.

"What?" she asked and looked up to him, confused.

"The papers are for me and *Nic.*"

"Yea," she replied slowly and slightly annoyed.

The small, forced smile on her face quickly faded as she looked down at the stack of jumbled papers and realized she had to sort through it.

"Here," Casimir said smoothly and took the papers from her with a smile. "I'll put these back in order for you, I'm sure you have more important things to attend to."

"Oh, thanks! That'd be a huge help!" she said with a grateful breath.

"My pleasure," Casimir said as he leaned in close to her.

He took the remainder of the papers from her hands before she turned and consumed herself in her work.

As he headed back to his desk, he shoved the stack into the arms of Nicolai and said, "Have fun.

# Chapter 3
## *A Guy Like That*

A few weeks passed, and the two men had proven useful to Liana, but she didn't feel the need to let her boss know that. It was Friday, and almost time to call it quits when Liana made some final saves on her programs.

Jessica's familiar giggle sounded a few cubicles down as she approached Liana's desk. Liana turned in her chair to see the spunky redhead accompanied by a few familiar faces. They all carried on about their plans for the weekend.

"Liana, Marty was just telling me about this awesome new club he went to. I think we should totally check it out," Jessica said while she grinned at Marty, a short and scrawny build, with chin-length brown curls.

"Great! What's it called?" Liana asked.

She was more than happy to tag along with the bunch; it had been a challenging week, and she was ready to kick off the weekend. Not to mention, Marty had talked to Liana previously about his fondness for Jessica, and they knew she would go along anywhere if she knew Liana was going too.

"Jackster," Marty said and grinned at Liana, thankful that she would entertain his ideas to go out with Jessica. "It's an awesome new bar, and they have a great DJ."

Liana looked at Jessica, who seemed nervous. Liana assumed it was partially from being skeptical that she wouldn't want to go to any new spots. She looked back at Marty, and urged him to go on.

Marty caught her eye and continued enthusiastically, "And hell, drinks are on-"

"You guys going out tonight?" Casimir said casually as he leaned around the cubicle wall.

Jessica practically swooned as she caught sight of him. Liana knew Jessica had been trying to connect with Casimir, and she didn't want that to ruin Marty's chances.

"Maybe, haven't decided yet," Liana said dismissively to Casimir.

"Ah, just wondering where you were off to," he stated indifferently but his gaze never shifted from Liana. "As for myself, I am thinking of going to this one club. It's ahead of its time, a little out of the way, but trust me; the DJ keeps this place packed and going late. Course, it's hard to get in, but I bet I can pull a few strings if you guys wanted to go."

Casimir grinned down to Jessica. She instantly shot Liana a look as if to say, *If you bail on this, I'll never forgive you.*

"Well, I don't know," Liana retorted while she grasped at straws as she tried to avoid issues between Casimir and Marty.

"I'll even buy!" he said, slightly louder.

The small group of people that gathered around Liana's desk cheered. She rolled her eyes, though no one took notice.

"So, where is this place anyhow?" Liana asked, and quickly thought about excuses they could use; maybe get lost, or go to the wrong club.

As if reading her mind, Casimir countered, "Oh, don't worry about that, you'll probably get lost. We can all meet at Carita's and take a car from there."

"Awesome," she said slowly through the teeth of her forced, enthusiastic smile.

That was it; no getting out of this, guess she'd have to suffer through this after all.

*At least he's buying,* she convinced herself.

○ ○ ○

"I could really go for a guy like that," Jessica rambled on. She had been talking about Casimir for hours as the two got ready for the night.

"Uh-huh," Liana absently responded as she applied a coat of mascara.

"I mean really; he's just so – mm!" Jessica let out a feral growl as she walked into Liana's bathroom and followed it with an exuberant giggle.

Jessica's black heels made her significantly taller and seemed to bring on a renewed sense of confidence. Her short silver dress clung to her form, and gathered at her curves, accenting them perfectly.

Jessica turned to Liana, who pulled and tugged at her spiral curls. She pinned them back in various places as Jessica ran a lint roller over the back of Liana's blue and teal blouse.

"Hey, what happened here?" Jessica asked tentatively while she lifted Liana's hair to reveal several barely visible tiny marks on Liana's back.

"Uh," Liana said as she shook her hair, and caused it to fall over her back to conceal the marks. "Just some scars; I was in an accident a few years ago."

"Accident? What kind of accident? What happened?" Jessica questioned while she searched Liana's face in the mirror for a million answers.

"I don't know really," Liana said while she dropped her head slightly and walked out into her bedroom.

She pulled at her short, black skirt in front of a floor-length mirror that stood in the corner of her room.

"How do you *not* know?" Jessica asked while she laughed awkwardly, and stood in the doorway of the bathroom, eyeing Liana from a distance.

"Well, all I know is he," she nodded her head in Striker's direction, "found me in the woods after a bad car accident or something." She paused a moment before she continued at a rapid pace. "I was badly cut up from the glass, had no memory of anything. Striker's owner took care of me for a while. He ended up passing away and left Striker to me to care for me. The police were no help finding out what happened or finding any of my family. So, I just moved here and kind of started new."

Jessica stood there, and let her mouth hang open slightly, with an amazed look on her face before she suddenly said, "It's like one of those holiday movies! Aww, your Prince could be coming to sweep you off your feet at any moment!" Jessica cradled her hands under her chin, eyes on the ceiling in dreamland.

Liana let out a snort and rolled her eyes in response. "Right. I doubt that's how things would go down."

Jessica snapped out of her daydreaming state and looked toward Liana. "How do you know how old you are and stuff?" It was evident she was fighting the urge to interrogate Liana but was trying desperately to be polite on the obviously sensitive topic.

Liana half-smiled. "I kinda feel like a 25, so that's what I told them."

Jessica burst out with laughter. "Why not 21? Come on girl!"

"Right," she laughed with Jessica, "like I'll pass for that!" After their laughter passed, Liana seized the moment, determined to end Jessica's obsession with Casimir. "Anyway, what about Marty, he's such a nice guy." Liana had an uneasy feeling about Casimir and wanted to make sure Jessica didn't get caught up in whatever he was about. She sat on the bench at the foot of her bed, and fumbled with her black lace boots, while she thought to herself.

Jessica mumbled from across the room, "Yea, I guess."

"So, you should totally make a move on Marty tonight," Liana said while she shrugged nonchalantly.

"Wait. What?" Jessica moved across the room to stand in front of Liana with her jaw hanging open. "I thought you didn't like Casimir," she said while she threw her arms in the air dramatically, "and now you're calling dibs?" she asked sternly as her hands fell, and rested on her hips.

Liana sat for a moment, a puzzled expression on her face as she stared at Jessica, and tried to figure out what the heck she was talking about. Suddenly she realized when she pushed Jessica toward Marty; Jessica had thought Liana wanted Casimir for herself. *I'll do whatever I can.* Liana heard her own voice echoing in her head with the words she had spoken previously to Marty.

"I never said I didn't *like* him." Her eyes shifted to the floor. "Just... maybe you shouldn't," Liana said after a moment.

Jessica stood silent for a moment, and weighed her options, with an irritated look painted across her face before she replied, "Fine, let's go."

With a quick turn from Liana, she grabbed her purse from the bed and gave Striker a pat on the head before she made her way out of the room. They rode quietly in Jessica's tiny car all the way to Carita's, one of Liana's favorite restaurants, now tainted by meeting up with Casimir, whom she had to pretend to like now.

*Great,* she thought to herself as her gaze remained fixed on the car window, frustrated for complicating a perfectly good night out.

As they pulled into the parking lot, Liana could see a group of people gathered near a limousine. She caught sight of Casimir, who must've been telling a joke because everyone else was laughing full-heartedly. He looked up from the group as they pulled in, and Liana could've sworn he winked at her. She shook her head, and quickly looked at Jessica, who didn't take notice. Jessica parked the car in silence before she quickly got out and slammed the door. Liana joined her at the group that gathered around Casimir.

"Well, ladies, it was *definitely* worth the wait," Casimir said as Liana walked up.

"Let's see this amazing club you were talking about," Jessica said with a giggle, and turned her charm on as she walked to stand near Marty.

*Whew,* Liana thought to herself, *Jessica is back to normal.*

The car ride was long. To Liana, it seemed like hours. The car came stocked with various types of beer, and by the time the group had reached their destination, most of them were already tipsy. Liana and Jessica glanced at each other as the rowdy group stumbled out of the limo. Liana turned from the vehicle to look at the building where they had arrived.

There was a large crowd gathered around the entrance to what seemed to be an old warehouse. A roped-off line strung around the back and out to a dark parking lot. Majority of the people gathered in a dense group in front of the door.

People danced and drank outside, where a small bar was set up complete with a DJ and lighting. There were people of all types gathered around. Some adorned outlandish costumes with an array of bright colors; some were extremely pale with tiny garments of dark reds and blacks. Lots of the party-goers wore different contacts; she saw some with strange golden eyes that drew her in.

"Ah! We're here! Follow me, my minions," Casimir spoke from behind Liana.

Her gaze broke as Casimir laughed and pushed between her and Jessica. He grabbed their arms in each of his. As he walked through the crowd toward the door, the people parted and stared. A moment after Casimir passed, they went back to their dancing and drinking.

They reached a large oak door where two broad-shouldered bouncers with shaved heads stood cross-armed and blocked the entrance. After a brief look at Casimir, they opened the doors without any exchange of words. Casimir made a gesture with his head then stepped through the door into a dark hallway. The room beyond where they entered was pitch black.

"I can't see anything," Liana said when she got an uneasy feeling.

Everyone laughed and spoke so loudly they drowned out her words. She clung to Casimir's arm as he steered them forward. After a series of turns, they walked through a dark velvet curtain that revealed a large open room beyond. The floor they stood on had neon symbols carved into a glossy black material. Numerous neon-colored lights pulsed to the beat of the fast rhythm music. Lit up, quartz-like bars lined the walls that stretched far into the distance. Glossy platforms hung over the dance floor with catwalks that connected each of them and held an array of people dancing to the music. Alone, on a large platform high in the air above the dance floor, moved the DJ. People swayed to her beats while they packed the dance floor, and moved together in a tangle of arms.

"Well? What'll it be?" Casimir bellowed as he leaned against the bar and waited for the others to catch up.

The night passed in a blur of drinks and arms on the dance floor. Liana pushed her way out of the crowd after some time. From a distance, she saw Jessica in Marty's lap on a loveseat, in a corner full of places to sit. Marty laughed, and ran his fingers through her hair as she happily spoke. Liana smiled with triumph and turned to find the restrooms.

Weaving through the crowd of enthusiastic clubgoers proved difficult, but Liana finally found herself in a less crowded section of the bar where doors stood that read *Ladies*.

After what felt like ages, Liana was able to freshen up and quickly enter the club again. As she stepped back out into the dark, someone from the corner grabbed her arm. She turned, and pulled her arm in a circular motion over her head in an attempt to break their grip. The man roughly shoved Liana and put his arms up to either side of her against the wall.

"Well, well, got you… to myself finally."

Casimir, who smelled heavily of several types of liquor, was now inches from Liana's face. She turned her head away from his, and almost gagged.

"Wow! How much have you had to drink?" she asked while she ducked under his arms.

"Aw come on, Jessica told me about your crush on me," Casimir explained. Liana let out a laugh as she turned to rebuttal, but he raised a finger to her lips and continued, "I could tell from the chemistry between us; you can barely keep your hands off me."

She let out a snort and grabbed his hand from her face as she turned, pulled him along with her and said, "I think it's time to go."

He pulled out his phone and yelled, "That's what I'm talkin about! I'll call us a car."

Liana ignored him and looked around but couldn't find any of the others as she looked through the sea of faces. She could've sworn they were all gathered just a short time ago.

"They just left. That's why I was coming to get you," Casimir said in her ear, his breath hot on her skin.

Frustration rose in her at the thought of being stuck with Casimir alone. Her agitation grew as he moved even closer behind her and placed a hand on her hip. His free arm swept by her cheek, and pointed towards the door before he nudged her in the back in that direction. She shot a glare behind her before she hurried along. She wanted to get away from Casimir as soon as possible.

As she made her way to the door, she was cut off by a rather large muscular man. He turned and looked at Liana. His form towered over hers, with long black hair and a long black beard to accompany it. His eyes seemed to glow golden like Liana had seen earlier.

"Excuse me," she said while she tried to step around him.

He moved in her way and reached to grab her shoulder. Casimir stepped from behind Liana and grabbed his arm. Without a single word exchanged, the man turned and left.

"Okay…" Liana looked between Casimir and the man that disappeared into the crowd.

"Come on, let's get out of here," Casimir said before he pushed the door open.

When they stepped out of the club, the large crowd that gathered earlier in the night was gone. The parking lot in front of them was bare except for a single black SUV that Casimir made his way to. He opened the door and gestured for her to get in. She cautiously stepped up into the vehicle.

"Wow, what time is it?" she asked, surprised, while she looked back at Casimir as he got in next to her, and sat way too close for comfort. He didn't answer so she turned her attention to the driver, and spoke in a warm, friendly tone, "You can just drop me off at Carit-"

"1096 Fox Furrow Way," Casimir interrupted from behind her.

"You don't have to drop me off at my house. I'll just take a cab from the restaurant," she said to the driver.

Liana slowly turned toward Casimir, an interrogative look on her face. He sat back in his seat and leaned his head against the window.

"I'm your assistant, aren't I? It's my job to know these things."

She moved over on the seat, and pressed herself against the opposite door, as she tried to stay as far from him as possible. Liana pulled out her phone and texted

Jessica to see if she was alright, only to get no response. Her phone suddenly had a lot of interesting things as she tried to ignore the stare of Casimir.

After a long, awkwardly quiet drive, they arrived at Liana's home. The driver pulled up the long stone driveway to the front door. She hopped out of the car before it could stop.

"Well, thanks so much for the ride!" she said before she turned to walk up the path to the front door.

Her hand found her face with a pained expression spread across it as the sound of a car door shutting behind her echoed, followed by the car driving away.

"Hey, no problem," he said seductively.

"Casimir, please go home," she said, so aggravated that she didn't even turn around.

The sound of Casimir as he collapsed behind her caused her to drop her head. After a long sigh, Liana finally turned around to see his drunken form passed out on her carefully manicured lawn.

"Are you serious? I didn't drink enough for this!" she shouted in frustration before she left her mouth hang open in disbelief and stared down at Casimir.

To her dismay, her intrusive neighbor was peeking out from her bedroom window. Her tiny glasses slid to the tip of her nose while her mouth hung open. Liana waved at Karen with a grin on her face. She was sure she'd never hear the end of this. Liana looked down at Casimir and heaved a sigh before she turned to walk up the stairs to her porch. Pushing her door open, she tossed her black clutch bag onto the table in the foyer, then returned to clear Casimir out of her front yard. She nudged his shoulder with her shoe, rolling him onto his back.

"Casimir," she said as she grew impatient, but he showed no signs of movement.

With the heave of another sigh, she bent down, and grabbed hold of his ankles. Anger fueled her strength, Liana grunted and grumbled as she hauled him up the path and onto the porch, taking care to bump his head on each step before she pulled him into her house. She shut the front door and leaned against it, exhausted. Striker trotted into the foyer, curious about all the noise. He caught a glimpse of Casimir, dropped his head, and let out a low growl.

"I know," Liana grumbled while she looked from Casimir to her canine companion.

While she slipped her shoes off, she made her way to the kitchen. Striker growled again at Casimir before following close behind her. Liana leaned into the fridge while she looked around a bit, then stood as she grabbed a bottle and closed the fridge. The low growl of Striker rose from behind her.

"Striker shush" she said, before she took a drink and turned around to see what he was growling about.

There Casimir stood in the middle of the kitchen, awake as can be, and didn't even appear to be intoxicated anymore. She jumped and dropped the bottle. A clatter rang out as it shattered on the floor.

"Shh," he said seductively while he raised a hand to her cheek, and slowly caressed it.

"What are y-"

He cut her off mid-sentence with a deep and passionate kiss. She stood there, stunned, and stared at him. He grinned at her, and it was slightly intoxicating. Something inside her stirred as he pressed against her, and made her ache for more. Her heart raced as his hand skimmed along her back, and rested on her hip. He locked her tight in another kiss as he guided her toward her bedroom.

"You seriously need to lea-"

Her words cut short again as she fell backward. The bed met with the back of her knees, and caused her to lose her balance. In an attempt to stop herself from falling, she grabbed on to Casimir's shirt, but he was more than happy to fall with her. An eerie grin spread across his face from above her.

His eyes gleamed a golden color as he leaned in and whispered in her ear, "Soon."

She woke suddenly, breathing heavily as his words echoed in her ear. Her body tingled at the excitement of the dream, which quickly turned to disgust at the thought of Casimir.

Her face pressed down into her pillow as she struggled to move. Her body felt heavy as if a weight rested upon her back, pressed her into her bed, and restricted the use of any of her muscles. Terror came over her as she heard uneven, shallow breathing in her ear.

Slender fingers crawled slowly up her back and rested on the back of her neck before they pressed into her skin and shoved her further into the pillow. Her heart pounded rapidly in her throat as a deep growl sounded behind her in the distance. The taunting noise grew to a roar before cutting off suddenly and left nothing but the sound of blood as it pumped in her ears.

Gradually, she could feel herself being freed from the grasp of sleep and fear. She slowly glanced around the room, and looked for signs of any movement. It was pointless as the monster she heard was only in her head, trying in vain to crawl from her dreams.

Though she shook, she moved to the edge of her bed and jumped to the floor. Carefully keeping her distance from the edge of the bed, in case anything lurked beneath, she headed toward the kitchen. With each step as it carried her further from her room, she began to feel more at ease.

After a quick walkthrough, she could find no sign of anyone, even Casimir. She heaved a sigh of relief.

*He must've let himself out,* she thought to herself, relieved.

The shrill sound of her phone cut through the house. She made her way quickly to the foyer where she had thrown her purse and retrieved her phone from it.

"Hello," she answered hoarsely while she rubbed her head.

"Good morning Liana," Casimir's voice beamed from the other end.

"H-hey, Casimir?" she asked nervously, and tried to think of something to say.

"Look, I just wanted to say thanks for lookin after me last night and letting me sleep on your cold, hard floor," he said, so cheerfully that it intensified Liana's headache.

"What?" she asked, confused.

"Well, I came to this morning in your foyer and assumed you *let* me stay there." He laughed, then continued, "Seriously though, thanks. I'll catch you around." There was a click, and the call ended.

*I must've just passed out,* she thought to herself, relieved as a smile crossed her face. *That had to have been a dream.*

# Chapter 4
## *Car Issues*

The deadline for the enormously anticipated sequel game Liana's team was working on was fast approaching. Liana had mandated her team to work later hours to adjust the bugs still in the game. She made her rounds through the office, and checked on each team member who was diligently at work, fine-tuning every aspect of the game. As she walked past the test room, she stopped for a moment to watch Nicolai and Casimir assist Marty while they checked several levels of the game for any leftover issues.

Liana made her way to her desk, and plopped down in her chair, exhausted. She clicked through pictures on her computer screens, while she went over the final details. The clock mocked her with every minute as it ticked on later into the night and she seriously considered calling it quits.

Beyond the walls of her cubicle, she could hear a commotion coming from the entryway. Jessica had left a few hours ago, so there was no one to stop the comings and goings of the office. Curious about what was going on, Liana rolled her chair back just enough to see around the walls of her workspace. To her surprise and confusion, Liana caught a glimpse of a group of armed individuals all clad in black that made their way in her direction.

Liana wasn't quite sure if this was some competitive promotion from another developer team in her company, but she knew she didn't want to get wrapped up in any of it. The urge to be done for the day overcame her.

Quickly, she ducked around her cubicle and made her way to the stairwell at the back of the office. She scanned her badge on the access panel and pushed on the door, but it didn't budge.

"Liana," a whisper came from the walkway on the other side of a row of tall cubicles to her right. "Quickly," she heard as she caught a glimpse of the blonde hair that belonged to Nicolai.

Hesitating at the door, she rolled her eyes at Nicolai before she turned again to leave but was met suddenly by the enthusiastic group. A hand rested on her shoulder and belonged to a man whose long black hair and hooked nose were all that was visible beneath his hood. He let out a short mocking laugh as his grasp tightened on her shoulder.

"Hey," Liana breathed as the man's fingers dug into her skin. "Let go of me," she said firmly as a look of anger crossed her face while she struggled to pull away from him.

He grabbed her throat in his hand and shoved her against the wall. Liana's eye grew as she realized this was probably a bit more than a competitive coworker. As he moved in close to her, he inhaled deeply and met her gaze with a twisted smile.

"Easier than I thought," he said with a thick British accent; his breath felt hot on Liana's face.

He hastily shoved her to the men on his left, who pulled her alongside them. As she struggled against their grip, she threw a glance in the direction where Nicolai hid, but he was no longer there.

The room began to blur and spin around her when suddenly she realized she was back in her cubicle.

Imprints of her keyboard shown visibly on her cheek as she lifted her head from her desk.

"Liana?" Nic stood at the side of her looking on quizzically while he said, "Maybe we should call it a night and start fresh tomorrow."

She sat up and stretched with a slight yawn. "Good idea. Maybe we shoul-"

"Nonsense," Casimir said from behind her, and placed a cup of coffee in her hands that were still in his face from their outstretched position. "Nothing a little caffeine can't fix."

"If you're working too late, you can miss crucial details," Nic said while he took the cup from her hands and placed it on her desk. "We are so close to deadlines, don't want to miss something because our minds aren't rested," he assured Liana.

"The sooner we finish, the more time we'll have off to rest," Casimir retorted sternly. He glared at Nicolai as he picked the cup up and held it in front of Liana. His temper was rising; she could feel the tension between the two.

"Okay..." Liana stood and took the cup from Casimir then set it on her desk. "I think we *all* should call it a night and restart in the morning. We'll start earlier to gain the ground we've lost."

"Bu-" Casimir interjected.

"I'm not asking," Liana said firmly before she turned, grabbed her hooded jacket, and made her way out of the office.

As she passed a cubicle wall, she paused a moment while she stared at the main entry door, and remembered her disturbing dream. It felt so real that she couldn't help but still feel the fear. She doubled back, made sure that no one noticed her, and made her way to the stairwell.

Liana climbed hastily to the floor below theirs, quickly made her way to the elevators, and pressed the button. When the doors opened, she noticed Nicolai leaned in the corner by himself. He looked up from his phone for a moment to inquire about the pause. After he raised an eyebrow at her, he absently went back to his phone.

As Liana entered, she cleared her throat awkwardly, and leaned against the wall opposite Nicolai while she kept her eyes on the floor. They rode the elevator to the main lobby in silence. Liana nodded goodnight to the guard at the front desk and proceeded to the parking garage. Nicolai walked with her to her car as he had parked on the same level as her.

"Hey, Nic," she said as he fumbled with his keys at his black Cadillac.

"Yea?"

He stopped and stared at her from across a couple of stray cars. As her eyes locked with his, she lost her train of thought. She felt so strange around him, so secure, but she couldn't figure out why.

"Liana?" he asked.

"Oh-" she said while she shook her head and snapped back to reality. "Never mind, see ya tomorrow."

With an awkward smile at Nicolai, she quickly shut the door of her vehicle. As she sat for a moment in silence, she thought about the connection she felt towards him and wondered what it was about Nicolai that drew her in. A short blast of a car horn startled her and caused her to look up from the steering wheel as Casimir drove by her. He waved with an odd grin on his face. She waved back quickly then headed out of the garage, now eager to get home.

o o o

The team could relax now as they had met the deadline with a week to spare. The rest of the team could take a few weeks off for a little rest. The only thing left for Liana and a few others to do was attend a release party before their break.

The company threw a huge party at the annual gaming convention to announce the new game. Mr. Kohaim always brought a group of individuals from each team to show off to his boss. Liana didn't mind; it was a chance for her to have a few free drinks and see the excitement from the game she had spent years working on. She walked through the sunlit lobby of the main entrance toward the garage, eager to hit the gym. Without anyone to stop her along the way, she was able to make it to the parking garage in no time.

As she approached her vehicle, she noticed that Casimir leaned against his, just a couple of spaces over. He spoke on his cell phone, his head in his hand in a hushed voice with an upset look about him. Liana wanted to leave, but she felt the need to check on him, as much as she didn't want to. As she approached Casimir, he caught sight of her and ended his phone call abruptly. He sighed and threw his hands up in frustration.

"What's up?" she asked as she walked closer to him.

"Car issues," he said as he turned and kicked the tire on his ride. "They're coming to pick it up, but I've no way to get home," he said as he leaned his hands on the hood of his car and bowed his head.

"Um…" she hesitated a moment before she finally offered, "Hey… I guess I could always drive you home."

Regret spread through her as the words slipped from her mouth. She cringed at the thought of having to be alone with him the whole ride but didn't want to leave him stranded.

"Really?" He looked at her in surprise while he said, "That'd be great! I'll owe you for sure."

He perked up and turned to walk past her to her vehicle. She turned to follow him and saw Nicolai.

"Hey, Casimir, what's with the car?" Nicolai asked as he looked back and forth between Casimir and his car.

"Getting it taken care of. Just going to catch a ride with Liana here," Casimir responded shortly.

"You're on my way. I'll just give you a lift," Nicolai said.

Liana thought she saw Casimir shoot Nicolai a glare, but her exhaustion from the day could've been playing tricks on her.

"Oh hey, that's awesome! Thanks, Nic." She clasped him on the shoulder briefly and headed toward her car before she said, "Catch you guys tomorrow. Final formalities, then we're done for a few weeks!"

Liana rolled the windows in her vehicle down as she drove from the garage. The warm air and relief of the freedom from work brought her peace as she made her way toward the gym.

After an exceptional drive accented by her favorite songs blasting on the radio, she pulled into the crowded parking lot of the gym. For minutes she searched for a spot which built her frustration and caused her to contemplate leaving. After another pass around the parking lot, she finally found a space toward the back.

She grabbed her duffle bag in a huff and climbed out of her vehicle. As she entered the gym lobby, the same receptionist as before looked up at her and grinned. She could swear this guy never left the gym.

"How's about that training sesh?" he asked in an enthusiastic tone as he pointed at her.

"Uhh… rain check? I'm just going to swim a few laps," she said with a shrug and motioned with her thumb toward the pool.

"One day!" He laughed.

"One day…" she retorted and laughed awkwardly.

The smell of perfume and hairspray engulfed her as she opened the door to the locker room. Ladies lined the mirrors and gathered in groups in the aisles next to the lockers.

"Excuse me… sorry…" she said awkwardly and pushed past several groups of women who glared at her and whispered as she passed.

Finally, Liana found an empty locker toward the back. She let her bag drop to the bench and donned her navy-blue swimsuit. Eager to escape the choking aromas in the locker room, she quickly tossed her bag and work clothes into the locker, slammed the door, and walked to the hall that led to the pool. Liana pushed open the door to the pool area and exchanged the chocking aroma of the locker room for the strong smell of chlorine that filled the air.

The pool was crowded with swimmers as the lanes were cut in half to allow free swim. Children screamed and ran in all directions as their parents sat on benches talking among themselves. Liana stood near the edges of the pool, and waited for a lane to open when a whistle suddenly filled the air.

She glanced to the side of the pool and noticed a group of older boys who attempted to get her attention.

They called out unintelligent lines while they tried to gain her interest, each whistled as if she were a pet. With the roll of her eyes, she turned her attention back to the pool where she noticed a swimmer climbing from the water in front of her. Liana stepped up to the edge to dive in when the swimmer turned to her.

"Pigs; can't even swim in peace," she said to Liana, and shook her head as she spoke.

"Such a shame. No men around here either," Liana said and smiled at her.

"Right," she laughed, "want me to take 'em out for you?" The woman raised her fists as she eyed the catcallers.

She laughed with her and answered, "I wouldn't waste your energy."

"True," she said and pointed at Liana. "Well, see ya around."

Turning from Liana, the woman grabbed a towel before she walked directly through the group of boys on her way out. They grew silent while some backed uncomfortably close to the pool edge until she walked past them. Once she was out of sight, they were right back talking loudly with each other.

Liana turned to the pool, and dove in. The warm water surrounded her and muffled the chaotic clamor that took place above its surface. With each lap, she grew more relaxed and energized. Eventually, she pulled herself out of the pool, not wanting to keep the lane occupied for long in case someone waited.

The noise had died down a considerable amount, she noticed while she looked around on her way to grab a towel. She dried off as she headed back to the locker room.

Liana took a deep breath and paused to brace herself for the circus on the other side of the locker room door.

As she shoved open the door, she noticed it was quiet. Thankfully, the air was less crowded with perfumes and sprays. A colossal sigh of relief escaped her as she made her way to the locker where her bag was.

The release party was tonight, and she had to make a trip to pick up the dress Jessica had picked out for her. Dread filled her as she looked at her phone and saw that it was nearly 4 o'clock. The boutique would close in less than 15 minutes. She quickly finished drying and threw on some clothes before she raced out of the gym.

The clock on the dashboard glared back menacingly each time Liana searched for the time. She dodged around the traffic and took every back street she could find along the way. As she pulled up to the parking lot of the boutique, Liana could see a woman locking the doors.

"No!" she cried out as she threw her vehicle in park, and hopped out.

"Sorry, hun," the woman said as she finished locking the door and turned toward Liana. A smile spread across her face as she pointed and exclaimed, "Blue suit!"

"What?" Liana asked, confused.

"From the pool," she waved behind her and continued, "making all those boys crazy." She laughed and punched Liana playfully on the arm.

Liana laughed with her. "Yea, thanks for calling them out. Wait, this is your shop?"

"Yea, my closer had to leave early, so I'm just lockin' up. You need something?" she asked and gestured to the store.

"Sorry, I know you're closed," Liana said.

"It's no problem," she said to Liana as she turned to unlock the door.

"I just need to pick up a dress."

"Come on in." She gestured for Liana to follow her as she held the door open.

Once Liana was inside, the woman closed and locked the door behind her. She made her way behind the counter to a rack with a suit and a dress on it. Liana approached the register as the shopkeeper pulled a tiny black dress from the rack.

"Want to try it on?" the shopkeeper asked and held the dress up for Liana to see.

"Are you sure that's mine?" she asked with a horrified look on her face.

"Unless you wanted the suit?" She gestured to the rack, then looked down at the tag. "Liana?" she asked while she looked back up at her.

Liana groaned in disbelief and placed her hands on her head. The dress looked a few sizes too small for her and had barely any material to it.

"Any chance I can get that suit?" she asked.

The woman laughed for a moment, then after seeing Liana's expression said, "Come on, it isn't that bad."

"I should've picked one out myself," she said while she dropped her head, and thought about what she had in her closet.

"At least give it a try," she urged her while she walked out from behind the counter and towards the dressing rooms. "Come on."

Liana followed reluctantly. She was pretty sure she gave Jessica the right size, but she knew Jessica preferred a more revealing style than Liana was comfortable in.

With a cringe, she took the dress from the woman hesitantly and stepped into the dressing room. She undressed and held it up to herself while she looked in the mirror with a frown on her face.

"Well?" the shopkeeper urged from the other side.

"One second."

Liana pulled the dress over her head, fighting and tugging it at every curve of her figure. After a painful moment where she wasn't sure who would win, she turned to see herself in the mirror.

The dress fit, and it fit well; it fit each curve to a T. The black stretchy fabric hugged her hips and draped over her bust perfectly. The back of the dress was left open and cut dangerously low. Several tiny black straps held the dress on Liana's shoulders and separated off in different directions, crossing in patterns over her back. She loved it and hated it. It just didn't seem like her style.

"At least let me see." The woman spoke again, and startled Liana.

For a moment she forgot she wasn't alone. Liana pulled open the door slowly and stepped out.

"Uhh." The shopkeeper stood there with her mouth open, not saying much of anything, she just stared.

"I knew it!" Liana threw her hands up and stormed back into the dressing room.

The shopkeeper cleared her throat and followed Liana. "No!" she said before she cleared her throat again. "You look amazing," she said slowly and quietly.

Liana turned, and glared at her.

"I'm serious! You thought those boys at the pool were bad. Get ready!" She looked Liana up and down and cleared her throat again. "Seriously. You have to wear it."

Liana turned back to the mirror and stared at herself for a moment, before she placed her hands on her hips. "I guess I don't have much of a choice…" she trailed off.

"You'll kill it! Come on!" she said while she jumped a little and nudged Liana's arm with her elbow as she left the dressing room and shut the door.

Liana quickly changed back into her clothes and held the dress up for a moment.

*Maybe,* she thought to herself, *I can pull this off.*

Hurriedly, she hung the dress on the hanger and exited the changing room. She thanked the shopkeeper for staying over and exchanged numbers so that they could team up at the gym again, then made her way home.

# Chapter 5
## *Time for the Party*

Liana pulled open the front door of her home, and let out a sigh of relief. Though the dress Jessica picked wasn't quite her style, she was thankful to have one less thing on her list.

As she kicked her shoes off, she made her way to her room. After she hung the dress in her room, she turned to head back to the living room in hopes of a little relaxation before it was time to get ready for the night.

She pulled the pins out of her hair, and let it fall to her shoulders before she plopped down on the plush suede sofa. The large flat paneled television mounted above the fireplace at the opposite side of the room sprung to life as Liana pressed buttons on the remote. As she flipped through the channels, she saw nothing that really caught her interest. A yawn escaped her mouth as she lifted her feet, and rested them on the center table.

"Liana," she heard a faint whisper as close to her as if someone had whispered in her ear.

She drew in a sharp breath and froze. After a moment when she heard nothing, she turned slowly toward the direction the voice had come from, but her actions were interrupted as a strong hand clamped around her mouth. The tight grip on her skin stifled her cries as she struggled desperately to dig at the hand that gripped her.

"Listen." The voice came again.

Liana's actions ceased as she made an effort to hear through the shouts that emanated from the television. The man slowly released her mouth, but the hand remained near her. The breath of the man crawled across her neck before his warm lips met with her cheek. With a quick movement, Liana pushed off the couch to the floor, and attempted to get a quick look behind her.

The figure leaned on the back of the couch, cloaked in shadows, and didn't seem fazed by her new-found distance. She slowly picked herself up off the floor, and strained to see his face. It didn't take long for confusion to set in.

"Casimir?" echoed Liana's voice in the distance.

A grin spread across his chiseled face as another voice sounded from behind him.

"Liana, run!" She had heard it before, so familiar.

His face came into view as he bounded at Casimir. Nicolai grabbed a fistful of Casimir's hair and used it as a means to ram his head into the wall behind them.

Liana stood and gasped with her hands around her mouth, "What are you doing?"

Casimir's gaze fell on her, the same grin upon his face as she had seen before. With one swift movement, he turned Nicolai before him, wrapped one arm around his neck, the other around his chest, and with a wisp of cold, silvery shadows, they disappeared.

Laughter sounded in Liana's ears which startled her, and with a jolt, she sat upright on the couch. Hurriedly, she reached for the remote and muted the commotion on the television so that she could collect her thoughts. Her hand found her cheek where she had sworn she felt the lips of Casimir. Slowly, she stood and turned to check the area where she had seen the two struggling with each other. Relief set in as she realized that perhaps it was all just another dream.

Liana looked about herself and took a deep breath before she walked to the back of the house, where she prepared a shower. A short nervous laugh escaped her lips at the thought of letting a dream get to her as she did. Still, she looked around as she pulled the clothes from her body and dropped them to the floor. The warm steamy waters washed over her. She let the welcoming hot liquid wash down her back as she leaned her head against the tile. Before long, she began to question how much time passed before she decided she needed to begin to ready herself for the release party.

Her boss sent a car for the team, so they didn't have to worry about transportation. Though she was pretty sure it was so he knew they would arrive on time. Whatever the reason, she was thankful not to concern herself with the drive.

Reluctantly, she pulled on the tight black dress and quickly curled her hair. She pulled the curls to the side, careful to secure them behind her ear with an ornate black and silver pin. A chime sounded through the air, followed by the sound of Striker as he grumbled in another room. A short laugh escaped her as she rolled her eyes about his lack of interest. She grabbed her small black clutch from the table in the foyer, then turned to open the door.

"Well, hellllloooo gorgeous!" Casimir's voice echoed through her high vaulted ceiling; his arms remained open as if he expected an embrace.

His dark slacks and blue button-up shirt emphasized his deep brown eyes and chiseled facial features. Liana cleared her throat uncomfortably as her eyes rested too long on his smiling face. She quickly closed the door behind her before she walked past him.

"Too scared to take a car on your own?" she asked as she walked briskly to the car parked in her driveway's turn around.

He jogged to catch up to her and laughed as he shook his head with his reply, "I figured this would be more fun."

He reached for the door and opened it for her, but she took no notice as she walked to the other side of the car and opened the other door for herself. As Liana shut the car's door, she looked around and noticed it was just the two of them.

"Could've at least brought Nicolai," she mumbled.

Casimir leaned in close to Liana as he shut the car's door. "Oh, I didn't think he could make it tonight. Didn't he say anything to you?" He questioned while he looked at Liana as the car pulled away. "He at least left me a voicemail," Casimir mumbled while he pulled out his phone, and after he pressed a few things on the screen, handed it to Liana.

Nicolai's voice echoed back in a short voicemail, "I won't be coming tonight, will be seeing you soon."

For a moment she stared confusedly at the phone, before she reached out and handed it back to Casimir. She thought it was strange for Nicolai to skip the easiest part of their job. Especially with a month break afterward. Casimir shot her a glance as she reached into her clutch and withdrew her phone.

She figured she would try to get a hold of Nicolai herself to see if she could convince him to come or at least get an excuse out of him. The phone rang once and went silent. With an eyebrow raised, Liana redialed but received the same rejection. She slipped her phone back in her clutch and stared out the window.

"Everything okay?" Casimir asked without taking his gaze from his window.

"Yup!" she said with a fake smile on her face.

She had an uneasy feeling about the whole situation and couldn't help but sense something was a little off. The long drive to the city passed in silence. As the driver pulled up to the substantial convention center that the release was at, Liana perked up. A large crowd grew outside of the building. Liana was excited to get the night underway.

"Ready for the fun part?" Casimir said, and turned to her with a grin on his face.

"Of course!" she said while she pushed his head aside to catch a glimpse out of his window of the crowd that gathered.

After the driver came to a stop, Casimir stepped out of the car. He looked back and held his hand out for Liana to take. She took his hand and pulled herself out of the low car. Masses of excited gamers gathered outside, and eagerly waited for the party to start. Casimir led Liana through the crowd toward the entrance, where they stopped and retrieved badges.

"Alright! See ya around!" she said excitedly as they entered, and started to make her way to her right.

"At least have a drink with me before you disappear for the night?" he pleaded with her while he gave her a ridiculous set of puppy dog eyes.

"Oh my goodness, stop!" she laughed as she pushed past him and headed to the bar.

"Two long islands," he said, and motioned to the bartender as he sat next to Liana, "and what would you like?"

A laugh escaped her lips before she quickly cut it off and cautioned, "Okay, Casimir, watch it. No crashing on my floor tonight." She waved a finger sternly at him.

He smiled innocently with his reply, "No? That's okay; I have something better in mind."

She rolled her eyes, and ignored him as she picked up the drink that the bartender sat in front of her.

Casimir raised a drink to hers with his words, "To a long journey, finally coming to a close."

"And, many more," she added before she tapped her glass to his.

He nodded to her with a smile before he tipped his glass back, then finally asked, "So, what will you do with all your upcoming free time?"

She smiled, and looked down at her glass, excited to get a break from work. "Well, I'm planning on taking Striker for some time away in the woods. You know, go camping, get lost in nature…" she turned to look at Casimir, who wore a horrified expression across his face, "…smores and shit. What?"

"You would voluntarily go live out in the wilderness, no room service, no bars, tons of bugs?" he asked very slowly as he counted reasons off on his fingers.

She rolled her eyes, and faced forward with her reply, "Yea, the point is no people usually, and you can bring alcohol. You know it isn't just served at bars, right?"

"Yea, anyway. Well, I'm hoping to catch me someone nice, fly them off to some magical destination of their dreams and have a little fun." He said with a wink to a group of ladies far across the bar as he raised his glass. Casimir tipped the rest of his glass back then turned to Liana. "Well, I gotta make a pit stop first." He laughed to which Liana only smiled. "*Catch,*" he said, and pointed at her, "you around." He laughed again before he turned to walk off toward the restrooms.

"Barf," she said aloud to herself.

As Liana turned to the bartender, she raised her glass and mouthed *Long Island, please.* To which the bartender nodded.

"Seriously, though."

Liana jumped as the person sitting next to her spoke up. She turned to see the smiling face of the woman from the dress shop.

"Feel terrible for whoever he has his eye on," Liana said.

They both laughed together as the bartender set two drinks in front of them.

"That's for sure," the woman said as she raised her drink to Liana. "Here's to avoiding as much of," she gestured at Casimir, who now flirted with the ladies across the bar, "*that* as possible."

"Cheers to that," Liana said as she laughed before she clinked her glass and took a large drink.

"I don't think I ever introduced myself. I'm Ari," she said, while she reached her hand out to Liana.

Liana shook her hand and was immediately relieved to see her. "Hey Ari, I'm"

"Liana," they both said in unison.

"I remember from the shop," Ari said with an awkward smile.

"Want to get as far as possible from," she motioned over to Casimir, who now flexed to the group of ladies, "*that* ASAP?" she asked Ari with a laugh.

"Yes, pronto!" Ari turned and slid from the barstool, before she moved quickly from the bar area with Liana right beside her.

Liana and Ari walked around, and admired the fantastic job the team had done putting together the event. As they walked through, Liana was pleased to hear a lot of excitement from the fans. A commotion arose at the main stage where gamers competed against each other. Liana and Ari made their way over and watched a few rounds of the tournament.

Ari looked down at her phone with a disgruntled look on her face before she mumbled, "Hey, I gotta go make a call. See you around. It was really nice running into you."

"It was nice running into you too," Liana said with a laugh as Ari turned and walked off, disappearing amongst all the people.

Liana headed to the restroom and freshened up before she grabbed a glass of water and headed to the art exhibits. She wanted to check out some of the fan art before she finished her night off with the premiere of the trailer, and then she would finally be able to escape.

"Buy you a drink beautiful?" a voice sounded from behind Liana.

When she turned her gaze from the painting in front of her, she glanced over her shoulder to see a sharply dressed man with long black hair and a hooked nose approach her. He had a heavy British accent and walked with an air of confidence around him. As he approached, a waiter passed in front of him with champagne on a tray. The man reached up, and grabbed a few glasses in one of his hands.

Liana laughed, "I certainly hope you aren't buying those considering they're free."

He smiled at her as he moved past a few people, before he reached her and extended a glass. "Wouldn't that have been embarrassing?"

"A bit," she smiled, amused as she took the glass and extended her other hand to him.

He gripped her hand in his briefly then released it. "Name's Taevior."

"Liana."

"So love, what brings you to an event quite like this?"

"Just here for the party," she said, and raised her glass to him. "To you," he said, while he raised his glass to hers, let them clink and lifted it to his lips.

"Sure," she said with a laugh before she tipped the glass back.

"Care to join me watch the tournaments?" Taevior asked as he admired Liana's figure.

"Um, no thanks." She smiled politely at him. "I'm actually going to meet up with some people soon, so I need to head over that way."

"Aw, alright then. Well, I hope to catch you around later." He smiled as he raised his glass to her again before he walked off into the crowd.

"See ya," she said as she raised her glass to the back of his head before she downed the rest of the bubbly liquid inside.

Liana moved along the walls of fanart from previous games in the series. She admired the detail and love for the game that showed in each piece. She stood for quite some time at a monstrous statue dedicated to the game with a group of long-time fans. They laughed and talked for quite some time before her phone alarm chimed, and reminded her of the presentation for the new game that was about to take place.

Politely excusing herself from the group, she made her way to the main hall, to a stage set up with a panel of speakers at the side of a large screen. She came in at the back of the room as her lead designer, Marty, finished nervously introducing the trailer.

As the crowd cheered, she locked eyes with Marty and gave him two thumbs up. He heaved a sigh of relief and gave her a reassuring smile before he sat. When the lights went down and the trailer started, she could hear the buzz of enthusiastic energy rise around the room. Liana's excitement began to fade as the heat of the room set in on her. She used her badge to fan herself as the trailer played, but her discomfort rose as the persistent heat in the room pressed in. Liana made her way to the exit, where she stood and watched the remainder of the trailer.

Finally, the end of the cinematic was met with a thunderous roar of approval by the crowd. She smiled with accomplishment and nodded to Marty across the room as the panel began to take questions from the crowd. Liana's discomfort grew, and suffocated her as she left the presentation hall, with the hopes that some air would help her.

After a few minutes, Liana noticed that even distance from the room didn't help as she continued to grow hotter, and the halls began to spin beneath her feet. She downed the rest of her glass and placed it on a passing waiter's tray as she made her way to the restroom. As she entered the back hallway, she could see that the line to the ladies' restroom was unthinkably long. She sighed as she leaned against the wall, and tried to be patient.

After what felt like ages while her condition continued to deteriorate rapidly, she looked around and took notice of the men's restroom that seemed unoccupied. She rolled her eyes as she pushed past the other ladies. The sizeable plain bathroom had a few men gathered, to which she took no notice. She made her way to the sink and turned it on as she bowed her head and splashed some water over her face. Liana rose slowly and took a deep breath, but she felt worse than before, and decided she needed some fresh air.

"Are you alright, ma'am?" A deep voice came from beside her.

"Y-ya, I'm fine," she answered as she pushed past the man to the exit.

She made her way to the back of the hallway, where a door led to the back patio area. She pushed through the door and walked off the patio to a quiet parking lot. The chill air seemed to intensify the disorienting feelings that came over her. She reached into her clutch and pulled out her cell phone to dial a ride.

"You alright, love?" Muffled words came from behind her.

She could feel a hand on her back, and the sound of a vehicle pull up. Her vision narrowed as she kept her eyes fixated on the pavement under her shoes. As she tried to keep the world from spinning around her, she slowly lost the battle and collapsed.

# Chapter 6
## *The Dagger*

The world spun around her in a blurry fog. Disoriented and disconnected from herself, Liana felt as her body was pulled out of a vehicle. The sting of gravel while it buried itself into the exposed skin of her legs, slowly brought her out of her formerly unconscious state. Two hooded men drug her through a dark parking lot before they came to a standstill. They dropped Liana's arms from their grasp and she fell to her knees as they talked to a set of men in front of her. Her head bobbed to the side when she tried to lift it.

*Get it together,* she urged herself, *just long enough to run for it.*

The men in front of her all wore deeply hooded jackets of a dark color and masks that concealed their faces from Liana's view. They looked large in stature. Suddenly, the man in the middle of the group stepped forward.

"What have you done!" he spat angrily. He grabbed a fistful of Liana's hair and pulled her head back to examine her face before he continued, "I specifically said not a mark on her, look at this!"

He furiously shoved her head back down; the force knocked her off her knees. She collapsed to her side on the ground as her face hit the cold skin of her arms. Every fiber in her body cried out in pain. She tried to focus her attention on the man that stood over her, but he was slowly swallowed by the darkness.

○ ○ ○

The smell of iron and dirt filled Liana's head with each pained breath. Distant beeps of a machine rhythmically chimed in the distance. She blinked a few times, and allowed her eyes to adjust to the blinding light that emitted from above her.

"Just hurry up," a low mutter of a voice sounded from above Liana.

The harshness of his voice cut through the air and echoed off the walls. A fiery pain burned through Liana's skin as her consciousness returned. She attempted to lift her head but could feel a thick leather strap that ran along the side of her face, and held her face down to the cold, hard, metal table.

"It has to be identical as before," another man spat back at the previous from Liana's side.

"I can't keep her under anymore," the man from above Liana whispered across her.

Liana could feel multiple leather straps holding her in place as she struggled to lift herself. As her eyes adjusted to the blinding light above the man who stood next to her, she could make out the jet-black hair and face of Casimir behind a surgical mask. His invasive gaze met with hers, and she could've sworn he smiled.

"Don't move," he said with a laugh as he turned his attention away from her.

"Casimir?" she asked, her voice hoarse and barely audible. "Wh-what's going on?"

Through the haze and confusion, she could see another person stood next to him, and held a small book up. A glint of light caught her eye, and she noticed it reflected off a translucent stone dagger in Casimir's hand. The handle of the blade bore small, carved symbols, and had a golden tint that gradually turned to a white glow as it neared the tip of the blade. Liana quickly realized why they held her down.

"Please, stop!" she begged him, "Just tell me what you want. I'll help you! I swear!"

Though she struggled desperately against her restraints, it proved useless in her weak state as she barely moved a muscle.

He leaned over her, "You *are* helping me."

A short laugh left Casimir before the look of concentration overtook him again.

"Such complicated spells, so easily undone…" he mumbled to himself as he dug the blade into her skin.

With a scream of agony, she pleaded with him to stop. With each tug of the blade in her flesh, came a sensation as though acid poured into every fiber of her body. Liana drifted in and out of consciousness; it seemed to her as though hours had passed when suddenly the lights went out. She could feel Casimir jerk to an upright position next to her.

"Check the door," he whispered to the men near him as he felt for Liana's mouth and placed his hand over it to keep her quiet.

Liana remained there, her breath uneven and shallow. She closed her eyes in the darkness, thankful for the moments, however brief, that he was not mutilating her body.

Casimir released his grip on Liana as gunfire sounded from the hallway, accompanied by the cocking of a handgun next to her. Silence pressed in on her from every angle. Moments passed with only the sounds of her pained, gargled breathing that filled the air.

A hand reached through the dark room and clutched hers; it was warm and secure. She wanted to get up and escape this place, but with every movement came excruciating pain. Without notice, she suddenly felt several hands around her as they pulled on the straps that confined her to the table.

Gunfire erupted above Liana followed by the shuffling of boots on the concrete floor. As she slipped in and out of consciousness, she could hear yells and gunfire around her. She felt herself lifted off the table into a pair of strong arms that were careful to avoid the crude tears in her skin. With a breath of relief, she buried her face in the chest of the man. The moments slipped by in a blur and ran through her mind like a broken dream. She saw the sun as it broke through the clouds, and tried to pronounce its start of the morning.

Through the haze and breaks in consciousness, she saw several people surrounding her as they hauled her into a black SUV. An angel held her in his arms. They towered over her with silvery-white hair and gray eyes that stared into her soul and pleaded her to focus.

"We couldn't get the dagger," a voice echoed around her.

"Just go," urged the voice of the man that held her.

The doors of the vehicle when they slammed shut sent unwelcomed vibrations through her screaming flesh. Exhaustion set in as the comfort of moving away from the pain became a reality, and the relief was so overpowering that Liana slipped away.

○ ○ ○

A field of white flowers stretched into the distance, at the center of which sat Liana. Everything was so bright she could barely make out the details around her. Looking down, Liana noticed she wore a long white sundress. A crown of woven flowers rested in her hand; she lifted it to inspect it further. With a quick rush of air, a young man came from behind her and snatched it up.

"Hey!" she yelled as she got to her feet and ran after him.

Liana jumped at the figure and landed on top of him. As he rolled over, the light shone off his face, and illuminated it where Liana could barely make out his features.

"Fine, you win," he laughed, reached up, and placed the flowers atop her head before he let his hand linger on her cheek.

"You're such a goof," she said, before she got to her feet.

Looking in front of her, she noticed someone stood in the dark tree line at the end of the field. Curiosity pulled at her as she took a few steps closer, taking no notice of the man getting to his feet beside her.

"Liana," sounded the stern voice of another as he grabbed her wrist.

The fields of flowers faded around her, though the brightness remained. She attempted to lift her head to see where she was, but it felt like she had a ton of bricks holding her down. Struggling against the pain, she tried to turn her head, and suddenly realized that the grip on her wrist wasn't just a dream. She could see Nicolai's head on the blankets next to her legs. His free hand, that wasn't used as a pillow by him, gripped Liana.

*What happened,* she thought to herself, *and where am I? What is Nicolai doing here?*

Bewildered and confused, a million questions churned inside. She tried to speak, to say anything to him, but her voice was nowhere to be found. The pain became too much, and she slowly slipped away again. The bright light surrounded her still. Liana looked around to take in the scenery and noticed a large crowd gathered in the middle of a white marble courtyard. The white stone pillars seemed to reflect the moonlight that shone down on the group.

Slowly, she stepped down the stone stairs that surrounded all the people. Unable to identify any of the individuals in the crowd, she continued to move through them until she could see what they held their attention. She peeked over the shoulder of a rather short and stout woman to see a group of children in the center. They all stood there and chatted amongst themselves as an older woman in the middle read from a scroll.

Liana looked back at the group of children to see that they were being paired off and placed in a line. A small blonde-haired boy carried on enthusiastically to the girl he was paired with at the front of the line. They giggled at each other as the girl tickled the boy. After coupling each of the children, the older woman came back to the front of the line, where she began speaking again. After a moment, she stooped to the first two grabbing the wrist of the boy and girl in one hand.

"This is your given brother," she gestured from one child to the other as she spoke, "and sister. You will look after each other until a partner takes your place eternally. You must grow the light in each other; careful to guide each other from the darkness that surrounds our Kingdom."

She smiled at the two children, and as she released them from her grasp, a white symbol appeared identically on each of the insides of their wrists only for a moment before disappearing. Liana pushed through the crowd as she tried to get a better look at the children, but the room grew brighter when she moved, and she began to slip away from the scene.

Before she knew it, she was back in excruciating pain; every inch of her muscles burned. Liana used every ounce of energy in her to push herself up on her elbow to a side-lying position. In trying to focus on the people about her, the room swirled and spun, causing her to fall back on the bed. Nicolai was quickly at her side, laying a hand on her shoulder.

"Whoa… Lay down for now; don't move so fast."

His words seemed to echo in the distance as she turned her head slowly to look up at him. The light in the room was overwhelming, but she could see him nod to someone behind her.

"My angel," she said, and raised her hand to his face.

As her arm came into view, she could see a strange scar on the inside of her wrist appear as she made contact with his skin.

He took her hand in his, knelt beside her, and laughed as he said, "Hardly."

"Nic?" she questioned hoarsely.

He interrupted her, "Shh… You need to rest."

He placed a cold rag on her head; the relief seemed so overpowering that it sent her away again.

○ ○ ○

Liana woke abruptly; as her eyes adjusted, she took in the room around her. Above her were twisted, white canopy curtains that fell from a wooden frame of the bed where she lay. Slowly she rose to her elbows, looking around. The room wasn't as bright as it had seemed previously.

A dull light seeped through the drawn curtains to her right. Shafts of light peeked periodically through the gaps of the curtains and illuminated tiny particles of dust that swirled in the air about her. Everything appeared so defined and detailed.

Liana slowly reached for her back and scratched at the skin that cried out in agony. The fibers of the grey, cotton, tank top tugged and snagged on the scabbed wounds. She felt the movement of coarse fur against her arm. Quickly, she looked to her side to find a bundled Striker in the blankets of the bed. Her eyes teared up as she fell over on top of him, and breathed deeply his familiar scent while she embraced him.

Out of the corner of her eye, Liana noticed a short distance from the curtains sat a familiar-looking man, though she couldn't pin how she knew him. He leaned back in his chair, two legs off the ground. His dark, muscular arms crossed over his chest while his deep sapphire eyes focused on the television on the wall across from Liana. His hair, cut close to his skin, complimented the sharply cut features of his face. Before long, he took notice of her gaze and turned toward her.

"Nice to finally see you joining us, sleeping beauty," he said as he set his chair on all four of its legs and let out a short laugh.

His voice was deep and friendly. He rose from his position near the window and strode to her bedside.

"Where am I? What's going on?" she asked as she swung her bare feet off the bed to move into a sitting position.

"Well I'm Khius, nice to meet you too," he said while he held out a hand.

"Oh...Sorry," she said while she reached up from untwisting the black sweatpants that were twisted around her legs and took his hand.

With his touch, every nerve in her hand felt as if it were on fire. Every sense intensified as she moved; she could swear she heard and felt his heartbeat through his hand. He pulled on her grasp and yanked her out of the bed before she could let go.

"Come on. Everyone's at dinner right now."

He put a hand on her back and kept a cautious gaze on her as they made their way out of the room. As he grazed the skin on her arm, the slightest touch zapped though her as though electricity flowed through them.

She heard a faint whisper, *Man, she never used to be this weak. I wonder how much longer…*

"Excuse me?" she asked with a sideways glance at him.

"Did you fart?" he asked while he laughed jokingly.

"Uhh… no, didn't you just say…" she trailed off, confused.

He looked at her, a puzzled expression on his face and replied, "I didn't say anything."

With an awkward laugh, she rubbed her head and mumbled, "Must be the meds wearing off."

She looked to the ground, and questioned what she had heard. They crossed the large bedroom slowly. Her legs gained strength with every step, and by the time they reached the hall, she walked on her own. It felt good to get up and move around a bit.

"Man…" she said while she stretched and arched her back. "Feels like I've been out for days."

"Hah! More like weeks there, champ. It will have that effect on you," he said with a laugh as he patted her on the back.

"What will?" Liana looked at Khius questioningly.

"Oh, uh… Nic will explain all that later, I'm sure," he reassured with a smile.

Cautiously, she followed Khius into a long dark hallway where a warm glow emanated from the other end. As they reached the light, she could see the hall continued, looking identical from the corridor where she had been. Khius led her to her left, where light poured into the dark hallway from a large open staircase.

Clinging to the railing for balance, she gradually followed him. The intricately carved, cherry wooden banister led her into a large, open foyer. As she reached the bottom of the stairs, Khius left her side. Laughter and loud cheers met Khius as he entered a room that lay across the foyer to Liana's left.

The stone floors at the bottom of the stairs felt cold on her bare feet. Slowly, she walked toward the room while she adjusted her top and combed her fingers through her hair nervously. As she stepped into the large double doorway, the whole room went silent. Before her stood a large wooden table; gathered around it were many unfamiliar faces, a smile on each one. She looked over each person quickly before she reached Nicolai's at the end of the table. He stood with a smile and walked toward her with an arm outstretched.

"Liana! Have a bite to eat," Nicolai said while he gestured to an open chair a couple of spaces from his right, next to Khius, who had already sat and dug in.

She tucked her hair behind her ear and lowered her head shyly as she walked over to the chair. As she sat, she looked around, and took in the table around her. It lay covered in food like a feast; she suddenly felt famished.

Liana took her time and filled herself with a little bit of everything from the table. The food was magnificent;

it felt like she hadn't eaten in years. Everyone around her laughed and carried on joyfully.

Finally, after what felt like hours, everyone had all but cleared out of the dining hall. There were a few stragglers left, including Liana, who had taken the opportunity to get to know everyone. Nicolai came to her, and insisted she go back to bed to get some rest. She didn't feel like getting back in that bed anytime soon, even though she was quite exhausted.

As they entered the foyer, a young woman stepped in front of the two, and blocked their path with her thick, curvaceous frame. She was the same height as Liana but had a powerful demeanor about her. The woman had thick, shoulder-length, brown hair that was tied back in a low ponytail. Her light blue eyes demanded Liana's attention and complimented her mocha skin.

"Hey there, I'm Arietta," she said enthusiastically as she grabbed Liana's hand in hers and gave it a stern handshake. "Come on Nic; she's been horizontal for weeks. At least show her around the place," she suggested while she gave him a playful punch on the shoulder and winked at Liana.

Liana mouthed the words, "Thank you," to Arietta with a grin.

Arietta scrunched her nose up and smiled before she turned and walked away.

"Great, now I'll have two of you pickin on me!" he shouted and threw his arms up dramatically. "Come on," he murmured, not wanting Arietta to hear that he was doing something she suggested.

He turned and walked quickly to his right, to a hallway that led toward the kitchen. A few men leaned on a large marble island in the middle of the kitchen, and spoke exuberantly to Khius. He winked at Liana, which made her blush as she turned her gaze to the floor. Nicolai ushered her out of a sliding door at the back of the kitchen.

"Here's a pool," he said while he gestured to the pool that lay just outside the kitchen as he shut the sliding glass door. "Ready to rest a bit now?"

She laughed and walked past him, looking briefly over the sizable in-ground pool. Small lights lined tiles that created a pattern around the edges of the pool. A few feet of stone served as a sunbathing area that surrounded the tiles and led to low shrubs and vines, all adorned with small blue flowers. She stopped for a moment and smelled the tiny flowers before she continued on a dirt path the led past them.

After a short time on the path, she reached a point where it branched off. Nicolai spoke from behind her, "To the right, are stables and training grounds. If you go left, that leads to a path that loops the house. Straight, you can eventually get to a nice getaway spot I'll have to take you some time when it's a little lighter out."

"Aw," she pouted with a pitiful look on her face as she turned toward him.

"Nope," he said while he shook his head.

"What?" she asked with an innocent smile.

"It's getting dark out, so, for now, we need to stay inside. I won't make you go back to bed, but you at least have to stay inside," he said while he stepped behind her and gently placing a hand on her back.

"*Make* me go back to bed?" she asked softly under a laugh.

"Don't tempt me," he said playfully.

"You won't get off so easily next time," she warned jokingly before she knocked into him with her elbow and headed back in the direction of the house.

She stopped at a stone bench that lay by the hedge and sat for a moment.

"What're all these people here for anyway? Where is *here* exactly? What even happened to me?" So many questions swarmed in her head, and she couldn't help but spew them out.

"You've always been so straightforward," he said, smiling down at her. After looking over her irritated face, his smile faded, and he continued slowly, "Well, everyone here has vowed to protect you."

"Is that *really* necessary? And what do you mean *always* been so eager? We haven't even known each other that long," she said with a half-laugh.

"Completely necessary, and we have known each other for quite some time actually," he said slowly. After a pause, he continued with a bit of hesitation, "See, we come from another realm. We grew up together. Our people have certain…" He stared off into the distance as if the word he was searching for could be found in the distant tree line before he continued, "powers. That is what those men were doing to you, trying to put that power back in you."

"Casimir," she said and looked at Nicolai suddenly; he nodded in reply. "I knew there was something off about him."

"I thought if I was close enough, he wouldn't try anything," Nicolai said and dropped his head as if defeated.

"Why can't I remember any of this *other realm* stuff?" she asked, gaze fixed on Nicolai as she thought back to her first memories on the forest floor, where Striker found her.

"Your memories are weaved in your power. As your power restores, your memories should also."

She let Nicolai's silence surround her for a moment as the information she was just given sank in. The sound of the water as it gently connected with the pool's walls while the warm breeze danced about eased her questioning mind.

"Our Kingdom is falling, and you're the only one left who can contain the power that could help us save it." The fading evening light reflected in his eyes as his gaze moved to the water. "There are some that are willing to kill to make sure the Kingdom isn't going to be saved. They want to use you for their gain. Do you understand?" he asked, while he turned his attention to her.

"No," she mumbled and turned her head away from him to the ground.

His words fell heavily on Liana's shoulders. Liana sat there, and took in his message, unable to respond for some time.

"So, what now?" she asked, so quietly it was barely audible.

"Now? Now, you should rest. Later though, you start training," he said as he stood and walked toward the sliding door where a faint light glowed from the kitchen.

A short sigh escaped her lips as she sat there quietly, deep in thought. From another realm? How could she not remember any of this? Nicolai was starting to sound a little crazy; this *all* seemed a little crazy. She didn't even know where she was besides in a large house surrounded by strangers. After a moment, she got to her feet and reluctantly followed Nicolai.

# Chapter 7
## *Bodyguards*

Her hand wandered through the sheets and found the well-known fur of Striker. Yawning sleepily, she rolled over to see his face on the pillow next to hers. The blanket slid off her hip and exposed the bare skin of her form to the warm morning sun.

"Good morning!" Khius shouted from the other side of the door before he nudged it open.

Liana sat up abruptly, and tugged at the blankets that were weighed down by Striker. Desperate, she pushed Striker out of bed and pulled the covers over her exposed form.

In an annoyed tone, she exclaimed, "Hey, you know, maybe knock first?"

"Oh!" Khius' eyes grew large as they fell on her slightly covered, naked form. He turned his back in one swift motion and called out, "Sorry... I… uh…" He shook his head and stammered, "brought you some breakfast…"

Liana glared at the back of his head, annoyed that he wasn't leaving. A heavy, drawn-out sigh escaped her lips as she flung the blankets off and got to her feet. The warm sun reflected off her pale skin as she crossed the room. Khius made an honest effort at keeping his back to her as she pulled an oversized t-shirt and cotton shorts on. Finally, she turned to Khius and cleared her throat.

Khius turned around with a large tray of food. He crossed the room to the balcony, and set the tray on a small bistro table that stood next to two iron chairs. The smell of biscuits, gravy, and pancakes wafted past Liana, drawing her in.

She followed closely behind him, and sat in unison with the tray as Khius set it down. He sat across from her, and handed her a plate. The two ate in silence while they stared off the balcony into the distance of the forest that lay behind the house. Before long, Khius let out a loud groan and leaned back in his chair while he stroked his swollen stomach.

"Little secret," he said as he stretched out. "You gotta have Deanna cook for you while you're here. I swear nothing else will ever match up."

He reminisced about previous meals as he caressed his stomach. Liana only half-listened as she stared into the distance over his shoulder. The dense trees stretched on infinitely behind the house. They moved and swayed with the warm morning breeze.

"Anyway," his tone changed, and caught Liana's attention. "You up? Got something to show you."

She looked down at herself while she pat her arms and legs before she said, "Uh... yea. I think I'm up. Not sure yet."

He laughed and quickly retorted, "Alright, smartass."

She smiled and looked back up at him. Her eye caught movement in the trees just beyond Khius' head.

"What's that?" she asked, alarmed, as she stood to her feet.

She could see the tops of the trees in a small area in the distance move back and forth violently as if something substantial knocked into them. A childlike giddiness came over Khius as he jumped to his feet.

"You'll see!" he exclaimed, excited as a child on Christmas morning.

He grabbed her wrist and jerked her toward her bedroom door.

"What?" she asked, horrified as she tried in vain to wiggle from his grasp.

"Don't be scared," he said through laughter.

"Striker!" she called out to the lump in the bed that was snoring loudly as Khius guided her out of the room.

Striker grumbled and finally joined them as they reached the foyer at the foot of the stairs. They reached the tree line in no time. Though Khius released Liana from his grip, she remained suspicious of his as they trekked through the trees. The deeper they went into the trees, the harder it was for Liana to not catch the air of excitement that Khius emitted.

"Are you going to tell me what we're going to see?" she asked, annoyed.

He laughed. "Uh no, it's a surprise, duh."

"What kind of surprise? Surprise, it's your birthday or… surprise you're dead?" She let out an awkward laugh.

He laughed too and slowed to walk next to her before he responded, "Just taking you to meet your new bodyguards is all. Calm down, dang."

"Bodyguards?" she asked in disbelief. "There's a whole house of people back there," she motioned behind them, "who guard me. What other bodyguards could I possibly need?"

Khius shrugged nonchalantly with his reply, "If you don't want them, I'll let them know to leave."

Liana stopped at a patch of dense vines that hung from the tree, and blocked her path forward. "Well…"

Khius moved in front of her and pushed the plants out of the way to reveal a large clearing behind. Liana could see at the far end of the clearing were two sizeable wolves who wrestled with each other.

"On second thought..." she said quietly.

Her mouth dropped open as she stepped into the clearing, eyes fixed on the huge wolves.

"Zhati," he yelled with a huge smile on his face.

As he motioned to the larger snow-white wolf, it moved playfully side to side, raised his butt, lowered his chest to the ground and nipped at the air.

"Purge," he motioned to the jet-black wolf who currently charged at Zhati. "They have been training to look after you."

Liana heard Striker whimper from the tree line; she had almost forgotten he was with them. He had stopped in the shadows and didn't follow along with the two as they entered the clearing.

"Aww don't worry buddy," Khius said in a sweet tone as he crouched, tapped his leg, and motioned for Striker to join him.

After a brief, reluctant moment, Striker bounded to Khius, unable to resist a second of petting. Khius embraced him and scratched his head and ears.

"They are here to help you, not replace you. No one could ever replace you. No." He said in a baby voice at Striker.

Striker's long tail whipped back and forth excitedly. A smile formed on Liana's face as she stared down at the two. Striker rolled to the ground on his back and begged for belly rubs, to which Khius didn't disappoint.

"See?" Khius asked as he scratched Striker.

Striker's head dropped back on the ground, and his tongue flopped out to the side. He jumped up suddenly and moved in front of Liana. The wolves closed in slowly on their group. Their massive heads sniffed at the air as they approached. Striker dropped his head in response and began to growl.

"Easy," Khius said gently while he moved between the wolves and Striker.

Though Zhati's large mud-covered head stood a foot or two above the darker head of Purge, Purge's presence had an air of intimidation. She left the side of Zhati, who looked at Liana, not moving his gaze. Liana nervously glanced at Purge, who crept closer to Striker, while her large furry paws dug into the ground beneath her as she moved.

Striker's growls continued as he stood his ground. Purge's size became more evident as she came muzzle to muzzle with Striker. Her head alone tripled the size of his, but he didn't back down. A silent, yet tense, moment was ended as the two touched noses, and a small electric shock was emitted from Striker. Purge yelped and jumped back, though her large fluffy black tail wagged. She made a playful snapping motion at Striker, who responded with a bark. Khius laughed as Liana let out the breath of air she had held in the moment.

"They were meant to guard the King. I was training them before he was…"

Khius' voice trailed off as he walked toward Zhati. He reached up with one hand and roughly scratched the top of Zhati's head.

"Well, I am glad they are here. They are definitely a valuable part of…" Liana's voice softened to a faint volume as Purge, who had now shifted her attention to Liana, approached her.

Liana cautiously raised her hand as Purge's idea of personal space dwindled to a non-existent status. The coarse coat of dark fur pressed into her cheek, and she soon realized she wasn't being eaten, but more so embraced.

She slowly moved her arms as far around the large wolf as she could. Her fur smelled of sweet flowers, honey, and earth, and was warm on the skin. Liana could feel the powerful breaths of Purge as she panted against Liana's neck. The moment was over before she knew it as Purge quickly took off and ran after Zhati.

"More than you know," Khius responded shortly before he let out a short whistle. "Wanna see something?" he asked with a grin so big it sparked curiosity in Liana.

"Eh, you know... this has all been kind of boring," Liana said sarcastically with an exaggerated shrug while she held back her grin.

Khius rolled his eyes before he let out a series of short whistles and turned to walk to Liana. The wolves took off running as Khius slowly made his way to Liana. The two wolves circled Khius twice as he walked then ran in different directions. Purge ran the perimeter of the clearing; she wove skillfully in and out of the trees that lined the edge. Zhati, on the other hand, ran back and forth in the distance as if he chased some invisible rabbit. Khius took notice and rubbed his temple in an annoyed fashion.

"Zhati!" he yelled sharply.

With that interruption, Zhati stopped abruptly, lifted his head to see Purge, then took off and ran in her direction. As he reached Purge, he collided with a tree at the edge of the forest. The impact left the tree leaning, half uprooted. Purge and Zhati collided with a clatter of growls and jaws that snapped in the air.

"Seems like you have some work to do..." Liana said shortly while her eyes fixed on the two entangled wolves.

She could feel the burning gaze of Khius fixed on her as she resisted the urge to laugh with every fiber in her body. Khius let out an annoyed sigh followed by a short, high pitched whistle. The two feuding wolves stopped instantly and stood. They looked at Khius and Liana for a moment before they bound off toward them. In a matter of seconds they crossed the clearing. Purge gracefully stopped short of the two, and strode a few steps before she sat to the right of Liana.

Zhati proved to be the perfect yang to Purge's Yin when he slid to a stop, the force of which, kicked piles of dirt and grass past Khius. Zhati clumsily stood and walked a few short paces to stand next to Khius, so the four were in a line. A small, soft bark from Purge caused Liana to look over at her. Purge looked past the two, at Zhati and let another low, almost inaudible bark out.

With that, Zhati let out a howl as blue-white sparks coursed through his fur. In a split second, the sparks spread from his coat to form a dome around the two. The electric forcefield of sparks sizzled and zapped as it enclosed Khius and Liana beneath it. Liana looked to Purge next to her, who was in the wall of electricity.

"The electrical current flows from Zhati to Purge, creating a barrier or bubble between them," Khius explained while he moved from Liana's side, to stand near the edge of electricity.

Khius' words echoed in the distance as Liana's eyes lay fixed on Purge. Her black fur took on a void appearance while it absorbed the electrical current as if it consumed it. She reached her hand up to the edge of the dome and could feel the intensity of the electricity and the heat it emitted. Khius' hand wrapped around Liana's wrist suddenly, and jerked it away from the barrier.

"Careful," he said sternly, as if disciplining a child.

He grabbed a tuft of grass from their feet, tossed it at the barrier, and it disintegrated as it connected with the shield.

"Got it," she said as she jerked her wrist from his grip.

The barrier dissipated as Zhati took off without notice and ran across the clearing, eyes set on a small rabbit that had popped its head up from a patch of flowers it ate.

Khius sighed again before he mumbled, "He still has a way to go."

"I'd say," Liana said shortly as she made her way toward where they had entered the field.

Striker followed close behind as they disappeared into the tree line, leaving Khius with the wolves.

○ ○ ○

Liana lay awake and stared out toward the balcony from her bed. Her head swirled with the events of the past month. Nothing made sense, and unease grew as she questioned staying any longer. She gradually lifted herself from her bed and crossed the room to the balcony. Dawn was breaking as she looked out and about. Not seeing a single person solidified in her mind what she wanted to do.

With quick strides, she crossed the room quietly, and took care not to wake the sleeping canines at her door. She tiptoed around their solid forms and crept down the hallway, noiselessly. With a glance around the corner as she reached the bottom of the stairs, she let out a relieved breath to still be alone.

She crossed the foyer in a few large strides before she reached for the door. Her hand lay on the large, ornate door handle to the main entry door. She paused for a moment to look behind her and to the side, while she questioned her actions.

"Good morning," a kind, soft voice sounded to her right.

In the room beyond, Liana could make out a young woman who lay sideways in a large armchair. Slender rays of the new morning light crept through the high windows and illuminated the reddish-brown hair of the woman that fell out over the arm of the chair. She spoke to the darkness in the room, not waiting for the reply or acknowledgment of Liana.

"The unknown is so intimidating." She paused for a moment before continuing. "The fear of not having power in a situation, it can consume you. You may try to take control of the situation. Go to great lengths to avoid the unknown, to remain in control." The woman sat up slowly and turned to Liana. "We weren't meant to have control over every situation," she said as she stood. "Our minds tend to remain fixed on ourselves, our own situation, not seeing the intricate web that we are weaved into." She walked over to Liana as the morning's light began to fill the room, and emitted a soft glow around the two. "You can think you are doing the right thing by taking a step, and you are really stepping into something worse."

"So, what do we do? Stand still?" Liana finally spoke timidly as the woman stopped next to her.

"No," she said as she guided Liana's face with her hand on Liana's cheek to meet her own gaze.

Her greyish blue eyes met with Liana's as an overwhelming sense of relief poured over Liana.

"You have a power inside of you," the woman said, now in an intense whisper. "Let it guide you," she said as she dropped her hand from Liana's face. "Ask the power inside you what step to take, what direction to move. Cast the fear out and rest in the comfort that this power, that connects us," she touched Liana's chest, then her own, "will guide you."

She turned from Liana and walked toward the stairway.

"Wait... uh," she realized she didn't know the woman's name.

"Liana, I know this can all be very confusing, overwhelming, and sudden. People are waiting for you. People's lives, people you may never even know, will be impacted by your decisions. I know that's scary, and it doesn't make much sense now, but it'll all start falling in to place the closer you get to the path you're meant to be on."

She turned and began walking up the stairs.

"Oh, and the name's Deanna. I'm always awake and around here somewhere if you need to talk."

A warm smile spread across her face as she looked at Liana before she turned to walk up the stairs. Liana leaned against the large door. The silence around her pressed in on her the longer she stood. With a deep breath, she finally turned around. The doors were heavy and required the use of her entire body to pull open.

As she slipped through the opening, she grabbed the outside knob to pull the door quietly shut before it opened much further. She paused for a moment and, in hearing only silence, turned from the door.

"Hey, there early bird!"

Khius, along with several others, smiled up at her from the bottom of the stairs of a large wrap-around porch.

"Uh... hey!" she said, and forced a smile as she rubbed the back of her neck and approached the group.

"I knew it! She just couldn't wait to get started," Arietta said excitedly as she walked up to Liana and threw an arm over her shoulders.

"Let's get going," another voice from the group interjected.

They all looked at one another, then turned and ran off while they shoved each other. They disappeared from the porch and around the side of the house.

"Come on!" Arietta yelled out before she smacked Liana playfully on the stomach with the back of her hand, "Last one there cooks tonight!"

Liana groaned, dropped her head, and followed. She rounded the corner of the house and caught sight of the backs of the men as Arietta past them. They disappeared into the dense brush and trees on a narrow path as Liana struggled to gain ground.

"Should've done… more cardio," she grumbled to herself in between deep breaths as she pushed herself harder.

"You stayed," a voice sounded from behind her.

She glanced over her shoulder to see Nicolai as he closed in on her.

"I don't like to lose," she huffed and pushed herself to stay ahead of him.

"Really?" he said in a lowered voice as he slowed to a jog.

Liana was happy to match his pace.

"Well… I guess… I decided to stick around for a bit to see what this is all about. Someone finally knows about my past. I'm not going to run away from that."

"Good."

A smile spread across his face as he broke into a sprint again. He dodged low branches and jumped over roots that crept up out of the path.

"You thought… I'd leave?" Liana huffed in between breaths while she struggled to keep up with Nicolai.

"I probably would've," he said with a laugh as he continued to gain distance from her.

She let out an annoyed groan as she chased after him and struggled to avoid the obstacles in her way. Just as she finally caught up with him, he came to an abrupt stop. She glanced back at him as she passed him and immediately lost her footing. The path had given way to a steep hill that left Liana tumbling head over heels.

Liana reached for every branch and root in vain. They moved past her in a blurry jumble. After a brief, painful moment, Liana came to a crashing stop against the legs of someone at the bottom. Nicolai was right behind her, though he took a more traditional way to reach the bottom of the hill. He reached down and offered Liana a hand to help her up.

An embarrassed smile crossed her face briefly as she mumbled, "Th-thanks."

As she stood, she took in the area around her. The sloping path she had tumbled down ran the perimeter of the training grounds and broke off periodically into separate paths that led back into the woods.

Halfway up the steep incline hung ropes that stretched high above the ground and connected with a winding net that canopied the entire training area. The nets stood high about the tree canopy and intertwined with each other to meet in the middle, above an open sparring area.

Off-shoots of rope periodically hung near the ground from the net randomly across the entire training area. Around the training grounds were different types of agility obstacles, climbing walls, pits, and ponds. Liana took a hesitant gulp as she joined the group of people gathered around the middle sparring area.

A short in stature but rather muscular man, with long black hair, pulled back in a knot at the back of his head, stood with his hands on his hips at the edge of the sparring ring. He closely watched Arietta and another individual struggle with each other in the center.

Liana lifted herself on her tiptoes, and tried to watch between two broad-shouldered individuals in front of her. Frustration mounted as she continued to struggle to see and before long, she let out a sigh.

"Excuse me," she whispered as she shoved her way between the people in front of her and made her way closer to the front for a better view.

"First one to beat Arietta gets out of training for the day," whispered Khius in her ear.

Liana had ended up right next to him, and his whispers drew the attention of the man standing off to the side in the sparring area.

"Ahhh Liana," the man said as he stepped out of the middle and made his way toward her. "I've been wondering when you would join us."

He extended a hand toward her as Liana moved to close the gap between them. His grip was firm, but thankfully brief.

"I am Antonio, your instructor," he said as he released her hand. "It is my hope that I will teach you enough to keep you alive."

The others chuckled softly as Antonio turned from her and walked toward the middle of the sparring area.

"Now, come."

He motioned from a frowning Liana to Arietta, waiting in the middle of the group. She took a deep breath, then approached Arietta.

"I…I don't know how to do," she waved her hand in circular motions in front of Arietta, "any of that."

Antonio laughed, and a few others joined in with him.

"But of course not, child." He motioned for her again. "You will learn."

"Child?" she mumbled under her breath with her head down as she made her way to stand next to Arietta.

Antonio opened his hand between the two of them. They turned and faced each other as Arietta raised her hands next to her face. Liana hesitated for a moment before copying Arietta's stance.

"Take it easy on me, okay?" she asked nervously, while she eyed Arietta's obviously trained stance.

"The enemy will not take it easy on you," Antonio said sternly. "Begin," he said in a quiet, calm voice as he motioned with his open hand and stepped back a few steps.

Arietta made one swift movement and caught Liana's neck in her arm. She twisted her about like an intricate dance. Before Liana knew it, she was in a chokehold on her knees, in front of Arietta. Quickly, she released her, and Liana reluctantly climbed to her feet.

"See?" Liana whined as she tried to back into the crowd.

"Again," Antonio motioned for her to come back to Arietta.

"What? Wasn't that enough?" Liana griped.

She dragged her feet and slowly made her way back in front of Arietta.

Antonio nodded at them. Instantly Arietta lunged at Liana, but she reacted this time, and jumped back from her reach. Arietta smiled at her as she raised her hands to the sides of her face.

Liana lunged this time and attempted to grab for Arietta's torso. Arietta was quicker and, in one swift motion, grabbed Liana's arm, twisted herself, and sent Liana flying over her, where she landed in a heap on the floor. Liana let out a groan and didn't move.

"We have much to do," Antonio said hurriedly. He walked off into the crowd and added, "Khius," as he waved his hand in Liana's direction.

Khius walked up to Liana, grabbed her arm, and swiftly yanked her to her feet. "Not bad!"

"Are you kidding?" Liana lowered her head embarrassed.

Arietta laughed while she walked up to the two.

"Don't be so hard on yourself. You can't get a PhD in elementary school," she said while she continued to laugh and slapped Liana on the back before she walked off.

# Chapter 8
## *Nightmares*

Liana looked around while she blinked until the haze about her lifted slightly and tried to concentrate on anything as the room spun in and out of focus. She looked down and wiggled her toes against strange white leathery shoes. Soft material wrapped under her feet before it crossed over the tops, around her ankles, and finally stopped at her knees. The laces of her sandals led to white leggings and a golden blouse, that fell to her thighs and gathered on her sides.

As she focused on her surroundings, she noticed she stood on a bed of beautiful, tiny, white flowers that seemed to open as she reached for them.  Her mouth hung open in awe as she glanced about and realized she stood in a whole field of them.

She could see the end of the area across from her only a few feet from where she stood. There were many large trees at the end of the field. It was very dark beyond them as if night had fallen behind the tree line and consumed all the light. It left Liana unable to make out anything past the first trees.

Hesitant to explore any further in that direction, she took a step backward. She felt as though it were wrong or forbidden. It was as if the trees were a border that wasn't meant to be crossed. After a moment longer, curiosity overcame her as she took a few steps closer and peered into the darkness beyond.

Something moved; from what she could see, it was a person. Her eyes narrowed as she took another step toward the shadows. The playful chuckle of a man echoed from the other side from the figure she couldn't quite make out.

An uneasy feeling came over her, and she took a tentative step backward just as a hand reached out from the shadows and grabbed ahold of her. The shadows fell upon her and consumed her. They nearly blinded her. She felt herself land against the solid form of the shadowy man. He embraced her against his chest as he rested against a tree and laughed. She looked up at his face and tried to let her eyes adjust to the darkness, but everything melted away.

Her eyes opened, and she found herself in her bed, barely able to move while she stared up at the ceiling. It was dark, but she could make out the white drapes that crossed over the poles of the four-poster bed. It took a few moments for Liana to remember where she was. A small thought crept up in her; she wished she would wake from this incessant nightmare she was thrown into. Gradually she let out a sigh, sat up, and slid out of her bed before she walked the short distance to the balcony.

Her hand ran along the cold stone banister as the warm night's breeze rushed past her. She looked up at the moon. With a deep breath, she took in the sweet air and peace of the night as she thought on the dream. Her eyes closed as it replayed. Could such a beautiful place really exist?

Maybe these were memories, and she could find that field again. A shiver traveled up her spine as she recalled the shadows, the darkness, that person; that face she could never focus on. Her head dropped in the palms of her hands as she leaned her elbows against the balcony railing.

The moonlight reflected off the rippling surface of the water below and caught her eye. Someone was below her in the pool. The side of someone's arms could be seen as they rested on the edge of the pool's surface. Liana placed her chin in her palm as she backed up slightly, and hoped they couldn't see her.

She closed her eyes, and inhaled the breeze as it danced playfully in her hair and ruffled her short cotton nightshirt. Like waves on a beach, the gentle echo of the wind as it crashed through the treetops calmed her and helped her previously uneasy state melt away. The movement of water hit her ears as she opened her eyes to see that the late-night swimmer below had begun to swim laps. She was curious who was up this late but remained silent and watched them just a while longer.

On one of their laps, they looked up and briefly met Liana's gaze. She instantly realized it was Nicolai below. She dropped immediately, ducked behind the railing, and hoped he hadn't noticed her. Her hand met her head that shook in embarrassment. Before long, she could no longer hear any movement in the water below. Slowly, her head poked over the top of the railing to reveal that the late-night swimmer was gone. Embarrassed at being caught in her peeping state, she turned to go back to her room.

Her feet drug as she tiredly made her way to her bed. The exhaustion set in on her body; she wished it would consume her mind too. She fell face-first onto her fluffy bedspread. As the comforter blotted out the sparse light in the room from her vision, her mind raced to recall the events that transpired.

Repeatedly she recalled the moonlight reflecting off the glistening water that rippled across the toned arms of

Nicolai. Tauntingly, her mind continuously replayed him when he glanced up at her, and their eyes met. Liana let out a frustrated grumble and got to her feet.

Through the shadows of the early morning light, she made her way to the kitchen in hopes that a drink and early-morning snack could ease her back into some sort of sleep before she had to wake and face another day of training. She pulled open the doors of the fridge and allowed the chill inside to wash over her. After a shiver jolted through her body and she still found anything of interest, she flung the door shut.

Her gaze immediately landed on the open backdoor that led to the pool. In the doorway stood Nicolai. Droplets of water cascaded from the low knot of hair tied back on his head, down over his shoulders, and to his muscular arms that lay crossed over his chest.

She stood there, mouth gaping, eyes fixed on his form as beads of water gently dripped down his neck and through the small tangles of hair that dotted his softly toned chest. The droplets teasingly raced down his stomach and met the revealingly clingy, short, boardshorts. Liana cleared her throat in embarrassment after her gaze rested on Nicolai's face, and she noticed he spoke.

"Sorry, what?" she questioned while she raised her hand to rub the back of her neck but quickly lowered it as she realized her nightshirt lifted revealingly high.

He half-smiled an alluring smile and cleared his throat before he explained, "I was saying how I forgot to grab a towel."

"Yea?" she asked, still mesmerized as the light glowed from the morning dawn and illuminated his form.

"So…could you help me out and grab me a towel?"

"Oh!" She laughed awkwardly and replied, "Of course!"

In a rush, she turned and shoulder checked the fridge by accident on her way out. She half ran, half skipped out of the kitchen to the nearby closet in the foyer to retrieve a towel. Liana returned quickly, towel in hand, and eyes on the ground as she approached Nicolai. She stretched the towel out to hand it to him, her eyes remaining on the floor.

"Thanks," he said gratefully as he took the towel from her and began to dry himself.

"Anytime," she said but her eyes remained on the ground as she rubbed the back of her neck. "I'm just going to head back to bed," she said quietly while she backed out of the kitchen.

Nicolai laughed.

"You act like I'm naked or something," he said while he cut extremely close to her as he moved between her and the fridge.

She laughed nervously with her reply, "I mean... you practically are."

A grin rested on his face as he glanced sideways at her and muttered, "Didn't seem to keep you from spying on me."

"What?" she questioned and tried to sound offended but laughed instead.

"You know it's okay; you can admit it," he said softly as he closed the door to the fridge and moved closer to her.

She backed up a few steps, and pressed herself against the kitchen island.

"I was *not* spying on you," she spoke as sternly as possible in her distracted state. "What are you doing up so late anyway?"

"I could ask you the same."

He moved from in front of her to lean against the kitchen island next to her. She put her head down slightly and turned her gaze from his direction, suddenly not as playful.

"Nightmares?" he asked after a pause.

"You could say that," she said softly.

"I have them too," he said, and turned his head from her to look out of the back door.

"What about?" she asked cautiously.

After a moment, he said, "The past, the future… you know," he shrugged, "boring stuff." He laughed awkwardly. "Maybe I can help," Nicolai said before he busied himself around the kitchen in silence, gathering a few things and eventually set them on a tray.

Liana stared off into the shadows that lay in the other rooms out of her vision. She wondered what it was Nicolai dreamt about that would make him want to not even attempt sleep.

"Come on," he said after a moment as he motioned with his head toward the stairs.

He grabbed the tray and led her to her room. He set the tray on the balcony table and motioned for her to sit. She smiled gratefully as he handed her some warm tea. As she lifted it to her lips, she drank it slowly as he spoke to her about some of his nightmares.

"At least you only remember fragments of what happened. I relive every detail, every time I close my eyes," he said softly with his head bowed over his cup.

"I wish I could remember my past; at least anything definitive," her voice was low and distant as she zoned out and looked across the trees in the distance.

"I wouldn't be so sure of that." He paused, and after a moment began again slowly, "You should start gaining some memories back as the powers that… Casimir transferred to you settle."

He looked up at Liana. She turned her attention to him and noticed a moment of concern on his face before he became his more chipper Nicolai.

"Come on, let's get you to bed," he said while he got to his feet.

She reluctantly climbed into bed as Nicolai gathered the tray up and closed the doors of her balcony. He made his way across the room, but she wasn't ready to be alone with her thoughts yet.

"Wait!" she called to him as she sat up in bed.

He paused near the door and looked at her as he waited for her direction.

"Um..." she swallowed slowly, "could you just… stay for a little?"

He nodded and attempted to hide a smile that grew on his face. After he made his way to the other side of her bed, he set the tray down and climbed in next to her.

As he laid down, she gingerly laid her head on his chest. With each stroke of his fingers through her hair, time appeared to stand still, and she was able to peacefully drift off to sleep.

# Chapter 9
## *Pineapple Chaos*

Tiny shafts of sun broke through the trees and dotted Liana's face as she bit into an apple. The warm breeze blew past her and brought relief from the hot day as she walked along the path. Nicolai carried on beside her.

She wasn't quite sure what he was talking about as she looked around and took in the details of the forest. Periodically she'd throw him a "yea" or "uh-huh" to keep him content with the conversation. Distance wasn't her intention, but the overload of the previous days had left her drained. She needed time in her head away from everyone.

As she looked around, she found her gaze rested on Nicolai again. His sharp features were more evident when he smiled, as radiant and energetic as the sun. He seemed to be in a particularly rare mood today, excitedly going in detail about something relevant to training. At least that was about all Liana could pick up on. The light would glint off his eyes every so often and catch Liana's attention; he would hold her gaze captive for an extended time and all but blotted his words from her mind.

"Liana?" Nicolai asked with a questioning look on his face.

"Yes?" she asked while she looked into his eyes, lost deep in thought.

"Ready?" Nicolai asked and looked at her questioningly with a searching expression across his face.

"Uhh."

She looked around at the faces that stood before her and noticed they waited in front of an ornate gated entrance to a giant hedge maze.

"Ye-" she nervously cut her reply short before she looked around again, and could see a map of the maze that Khius examined while the others with headphones in hand, tied each other's blindfolds. "Yea, of course," she said as she looked back for Nicolai, but darkness overtook her.

She felt up to her face where Nicolai tied a blindfold over her eyes.

"Alright when I say go," Nicolai's voice boomed from behind Liana, "place the noise-canceling headphones on and link up with each other. Once we confirm we're all together, we'll enter the maze."

Liana was unsure how Nicolai expected any of them to make it into the maze blindfolded and unable to hear, let alone make it out.

She didn't have much time to question the latest training shenanigan as Nicolai shouted, "Go."

Liana slipped the noise-canceling headphones over her ears to welcome an anxiety-inducing silence. Her blood pounded frantically in her ears behind a deafening ring, accompanied by the shallow draws of her panicked lungs.

As she reached desperately ahead, the grasp of a smaller yet firm hand gripped her and held her in place. She held still, and the grip eased, yet remained on her shoulder. After a moment, the person behind her gently nudged her forward until her outstretched hand connected with someone near her. She moved her hand toward their shoulder and repeated the same squeeze motions she had previously experienced.

After what felt like an eternity of awkward jerking and stumbling, she felt the breeze of someone to her left as they passed her and gently tapped her head. A few moments after the awkward bonk on the head, Liana felt the individual in front of her pull her forward. She reached with her free hand out to her side and felt the rough branches and tiny leaves of the hedges.

"We actually made it in," she said aloud to no one.

Her voice was extremely loud as it reverberated back in her ears.

*Wow,* she thought to herself, *super negative.*

Liana lowered her head in thought as she followed along the twisting maze with the others. It wasn't long before they came to a jerking halt, and Liana knocked into the back of the individual who was in her grip. She patted their shoulder awkwardly while she tried to apologize in some aspect, but then she felt creepy, so she let go. Just as she released their shoulder, the person moved out of her reach.

"Wait!" she shouted and immediately flinched at her voice as it echoed loudly in her head.

Panic crept up again, like a dark, sinister evil that lingered in the distance waiting for the opportune moment to consume her. Her breaths became uneven as she frantically felt in front of her for any fiber of a shirt or strand of hair that would connect her back to the group. She took a few steps forward as something moved past her outstretched hand and barely grazed her fingertips. Instantly, she withdrew her hand. Whatever had just moved past moved at a quick speed, and by the feel of the air that rushed by Liana from the object, it was also a bit heavy.

Liana thought for a moment while she took a few deep breaths. The panic shrank away to the shadows as her curiosity set in. She slowly reached her hand out in front of her and felt the breeze of the object when it rushed by. It made a pendulum like back-and-forth motion in front of her and was quite slow.

When she reached up to her shoulder, she released the grip of the individual behind her. She stretched her hand out again, and when the object passed, she jumped. A huge sigh of relief escaped Liana as she felt the rush of the object sweep across her back and narrowly miss her rear.

Suddenly, someone grabbed her arm and jerked her forward just as she felt another individual knock into her back. They placed her hand on the shoulder in front of her just as the hand of the person behind her found her shoulder. One after another, they shuffled along until they walked at a steady pace again. Liana began to slow as exhaustion set in, and her stomach rumbled.

*Just an apple for breakfast,* she thought, frustrated, and distracted by her hunger pains, *was probably not the best decision.*

The others in front of her picked up their pace; Liana felt her arm tug, and her grip loosen several times as she began to fall behind. She sighed, and the echo of her frustration reverberated annoyingly in the noise-canceling headphones.

Before long, the group came to a stop. Liana stood silently and tried to listen in vain for any sign of what transpired in front of her. Moments turned to minutes and minutes to what felt like hours as Liana shifted her weight from foot to foot and grew more impatient.

Unexpectedly, she felt another hand on hers that pulled her from the shoulder she gripped, down toward the ground. They guided her down to a wire near her knees and rested there for a moment before they pulled her hand to the ground and let go. For a while, she remained there crouched awkwardly, a bit confused. Her fingers intertwined with the blades of grass playfully as she sat in thought. She raised her hand to the wire again and slid her fingers across. The wire seemed to run a few feet in both directions and had several sharp barbs along the way.

Her heart thumped heavily in her ears as she heaved another sigh and reached for the hand on her shoulder. Mimicking the actions of the person in front of her, she guided the other person's hand to the wire then to the ground. Liana pat the person's shoulder twice and gave a nervous chuckle to herself as she lowered her body to the ground. She reached up for the wire to see how close it was and noticed she had a pretty decent space to wiggle under.

Without wasting time, she pulled herself along under the wire. It didn't take long before Liana felt the side of her hand brush up against the boot of someone in front of her. A breath of relief escaped Liana as a grin spread across her face. She pulled herself along while she dug her feet into the grass and pushed off as she could.

Liana wondered if the group behind her caught up yet. She turned around and paused while she lifted her head slightly. After a few seconds, she felt a hand brush the heel of her shoe. A grin spread across her face again as she turned to move. As she pulled herself forward, her bun tugged roughly, and snagged in the barbed wire.

*Seriously,* she thought to herself in frustration while she reached up to free her bun of the wire's grasp.

After a moment of painful tugs, she was able to get her hair loose. She lowered herself as low to the ground as she could and began to push herself forward with her legs again. After a short distance, Liana felt the breeze of someone as they moved beside her head, and suddenly a hand gripped her outstretched arm. Another hand settled on her back and urged her forward. She pulled herself a little further before the hand on her arm yanked her to a standing position.

Liana looked down as she brushed herself off and chuckled as she remembered she couldn't see. She lifted her arms to feel around for the others. Her arm connected painfully with someone else's. They grabbed her and turned her around to guide her to the shoulder of an individual right behind her.

She stretched and twisted her back as she stood there and waited. Before long, a hand found her shoulder and moments after, she felt the breeze of someone as they walked by. Their hand glided over Liana's outstretched arm, over her hand and on to the next person. A thankfulness rose in Liana, when suddenly, the person in front of her tugged her forward. Shortly after, they walked again.

Liana listened to the rhythmic draws of her breath as she reached out with her free hand to feel the hedge next to her. The rough branches and tiny leaves slipped through her fingertips as they walked on. She could feel the warm sun as it rose above her head and warmed her bare shoulders.

Her stomach gurgled as hunger nudged her memory again. Liana was very thankful for the headphones at this point, so the others didn't have to hear what she assumed was a very loud performance featuring her stomach. Hoping to pick up the pace, she gently pushed on the person in front of her. Just as she did, they stopped. A hand was on hers again as it slowly guided her forward. She moved her feet along the ground and tried to feel out.

After a moment, she felt the ground disappear as her foot slid from the edge to find only air. With a quick step backward, she released the hand in front of her. She reached out with her foot again, felt for the edge, and slid her foot out in front of her. As she stepped close to the edge, she reached out with her hand and foot to see if she could feel the other side. When the air was the only thing her foot landed on, she assumed she needed to jump across.

Shaking her head, she thought to herself how she ended up here, about to jump across some unknown size of a pit, blindfolded and unable to hear. With a loud laugh, she took a breath and guided the person behind her to her right so they could feel the edge. She then stuck her foot out and felt one last time before she backed up a few paces. With some calculated steps, she jumped over the gap and reached the other side with ease. Stumbling forward, she collided harshly with the solid form of someone in front of her, and sent them tumbling forward.

"Sorry!" she yelled out in vain before she sighed at herself in frustration.

When she reached down to lift herself to her feet, she could feel the edge of the ground where the pit was, just beyond where she landed. Liana reached out in front of her and quickly found a person. After she rested her hand on their shoulder, she turned and extended her free hand while she waited for the person behind her to arrive. A hand found hers after a moment, and she brought it to her shoulder before she turned to face forward. They moved slowly forward and gradually returned to a decent pace.

Liana's breaths became more rapid and she noticed they were now moving at a fast pace. Occasionally she would graze the heel of the person in front of her. She tried to match their strides as she felt the movement of their shoulders. Just as she got the hang of it, their pace began to slow until they were at yet another standstill. She groaned in frustration, and her patience dwindled as she longed for this whole ordeal to end. Suddenly someone tugged at her hair which caused her to reach up and grab their wrist. Just then, her headphones were yanked from her head.

"Take off your blindfold dummy," Khius said with a laugh.

She sighed, rather annoyed as she reached up and yanked her blindfold down around her neck. Blinded by the bright afternoon sun, she looked around at everyone while she let her eyes adjust.

"How fast did we make it through?" she asked while she looked toward Khius.

"We made it through," he said and laughed as he waved a dismissive hand at her inquiry. "Good job," he added before he walked off toward a growing group with huge grins on their face as Khius, the center of attention, went on about his epic pendulum battle.

Liana rolled her eyes, which landed on a table of food that sat off to the side in the shade. The others slowly made their way over, and she thankfully joined them. Liana sat next to Arietta, who had already made herself a large plate and sat back talking with Wes.

"Gotta make sure you grab enough before Khius notices!" Arietta laughed.

The breeze blew colder in the deep shade of the massive oak tree. Liana was grateful to sit back and soak it up while she listened to the various stories of the others.

"What'd you think of the maze, Liana?" Wes echoed from across the table.

"Oh." Liana had been lost in thought and was suddenly unable to recall any details of the maze in the slightest. "Uh…which part sucked the most?"

She adorned a thinking face to the amusement of the others, who immediately roared with laughter. Grinning thankfully at the group, she added a few chuckles herself, thankful to evade the question. After a moment, the others began to eat. All except Nicolai, who was seated directly in front of Liana and stared straight at her.

"Well? What part sucked the most?" he asked with a slightly intrusive grin as if he knew Liana wasn't mentally there with them.

Liana took a bite of her sandwich and held up a hand slightly to Nicolai for him to wait as she rewound the day's events in her head. She casually choked a laugh out after she finished her mouthful of food.

"Well, I can't believe you had us jumping over pits. I mean," she glanced around at everyone, eyes all fixed on her with confused expressions on their faces before she slowly continued, "that… can't… be safe. Why are you guys looking at me like you don't know what I'm talking about?"

"What *are* you talking about?" Arietta mumbled in a hushed tone as if no one could hear her through the silence.

"There was like, a huge pit!" Liana said while she stretched her arms out to her sides, and attempted to show how large the pit was. "I felt the edge with my foot and felt out for the other side and nothing. I had to jump to get across!"

"I don't remember jumpin no pit," Wes laughed awkwardly, "that's insane."

"That's what I thought!" she said before she laughed with the others and second-guessed her memories.

"Wait!" Khius shouted suddenly. "There was a *board* we walked across, probably sitting across a 'pit'." He started laughing as he spoke, "You have to make everything harder! Jumpin over instead of walkin across."

Khius continued to laugh, and even kicked Liana under the table periodically. Liana laughed for a moment then rolled her eyes, annoyed at how Khius could find it *that* funny. Khius made eye contact with her for a short second and glanced at her then the table a few times before he kicked her again.

"Everyone walked the plank?" she asked while she looked around from face to face as the laughter grew in response to her question.

"Aye," they all said in unison before deafening laughter erupted from everyone, including Liana.

"Wow," she said as she stretched back awkwardly.

When she stretched, she glanced under the table where a folded-up piece of paper caught her eye.

"I really do make things harder."

Liana shrugged, put her foot on the paper, and pulled it towards her as she stood from the table. She stooped, pretended to adjust her sock, and pocketed the paper as she stood.

Arietta slapped Liana playfully on the back as she stood with her and called out, "We still made it through, so who cares. Who's going to the grounds?"

A few of the others stood while they cheered at Arietta as if being invited to a party. Liana began to walk in the opposite direction of the others.

"Not comin?" Wes asked Liana as he stood from the almost empty table.

"Maybe next time," she said after she turned around to face Wes.

Wes nodded his head to her before he turned and ran off into the trees after the others.

"See ya," she said to Nicolai and Khius, who were left at the table.

They were in a deep mumbled conversation and gave a half audible "Later," in reply.

Liana gave a shrug and turned before she walked off along a path she hoped led to the house. After a short distance, the trees closed in around her which got her out of sight of Khius and Nicolai. Her pace began to slow as she fumbled in her pocket and, after a moment of frustration, yanked out the piece of paper. As she examined the paper, she realized it was a page ripped from a magazine. It was some cooking recipe called *'Pineapple Chaos'* that, according to the article, would *'Amaze your taste buds, whipping them into a fruity frenzy'.*

Her pace picked back up as she folded the paper and shoved it back in her pocket. It wasn't long before she rounded the corner, and the house came to view. Deep in thought, she made her way through the twists and turns of the house toward her room.

*Why would Khius,* she thought to herself, *so secretively slide me a recipe under the table like that?*

She knew he tended to joke around a lot, but this didn't seem as funny as his typical pranks. The door clicked behind her as she leaned her back against it. While she slid to the floor of her bedroom, she took the magazine page out again and examined it closer. As she reread the article, she noticed the '*P*' in pineapple had a small pen mark under it as if someone underlined it. She read through the article and saw several letters underlined.

Liana hastily got to her feet and retrieved a pen from the end table next to her bed. As she slowly sat on the edge of the bed, she wrote down each underlined letter along the side of the article. After a few seconds, Liana saw the message '*Pool 1 hour*' scrawled in the margins. A laugh escaped her lips.

*Okay,* she thought to herself as she glanced around the room for a clock, *this seems more like Khius.*

Once her eyes settled on the time, it dawned on her that she had no clue when Khius had given her the note. This was actually the first time she had looked at the clock in days. She heaved a hefty sigh as she lifted herself from the bed and made her way down to the pool to wait on Khius.

The breeze danced gently across the waters; it caused small ripples to cascade out and bump into the walls of the pool with gentle splashes that created a rhythmic melody in Liana's ears. When she closed her eyes, she drew in a deep breath, and listened to the breeze while it flowed through the trees. The cooling air of the sun set danced around her playfully; it renewed her mind and lifted her spirit. She heard voices in the distance as they approached, but she remained seated still. It wasn't until she caught the voice of Nicolai when it echoed to someone near her, that she got to her feet.

"Liana shouldn't be seeing that. It'll confuse her."

"I don't think you give her enough credit for what she can handle, Nicolai," Khius' voice cut through the air as it closed in.

Liana stepped from the stone patio to the edge of the house and leaned against the wall as she listened.

"How'd you even come across it?" Nicolai's voice lowered as their footsteps hit the stone floor that surrounded the pool.

"I understand you're just trying to protect her. She has a right to know more about where she came from. Show her what she's fighting for."

"Until she reads the wrong part and-"

"Look, Nicolai," Khius lowered his voice, and though Liana strained to listen, she couldn't make out much of anything at this point.

After a few moments of failed attempts to listen to the two again, Liana poked her head around the corner. To her surprise, Khius stood face to face with her.

She jumped back, startled, and shouted, "Geeze!"

"Eavesdrop much?" Khius asked with arms crossed over his chest and a huge grin on his face.

Liana rolled her eyes and peered quickly around Khius to see Nicolai was gone.

"At least I'm not passing serial killer love notes." She looked Khius up and down as she spoke before she took a few dramatic steps backward with her hands raised up as if she were afraid.

"Whatever. Anyway, you should get some time away from everyone." His voice lowered so significantly that Liana had to step closer to hear what he was said, "go browse the library upstairs for some," he looked around suspiciously, "reading."

"What?" She narrowed her eyes at him before she asked, "Why would I-"

A huge sigh interrupted Liana's speech, and Khius stared at her insistently.

"Did you not just hear all that?" he asked while he motioned behind himself to where he previously spoke with Nicolai.

"Right…" she trailed off and watched Khius as he walked back toward the house.

"Maybe try the top shelf."

As he spoke, he made a motion with his hand as if feeling on top of a bookshelf. He then disappeared through the door into the house.

# Chapter 10
## *Shocking Talents*

Dawn's warm light cracked rudely through the drawn curtains of Liana's room and hit her square in the eyes. She rolled over and begged herself to go back to sleep. After a moment of wasted pleading, she opened her eyes. To her dismay, she found she was still in the large comfy bed that lay guarded by a house of canines and strangers.

*Great,* she thought to herself.

She had hoped this was all a dream, and when she woke, she'd be back fighting the battles of pesky neighbors and micromanaging bosses. A loud laugh escaped her, as the very thought itself should have sounded a bit insane but instead brought familiarity and comfort. Liana rolled from her bed, and let a frustrated groan escape her. With a glance at the clock, she knew she'd be expected at the training grounds in an hour, and she knew she'd be late. Liana dressed hastily and attempted to be quiet so as not to wake the snoring canines outside of her room.

Slowly and quietly, she crept toward her door, and pressed an ear to it to hear if anyone was in the hall on the other side. After a moment of hearing nothing but snores, she slowly pulled the door open. A large furry blob plopped on the floor at her feet. After a moment of panic, Liana realized that the snoring blob of her guard dog was still sound asleep. She tip-toed silently over his solid form and ran down the hallway. At the end of the corridor lay a small spiral staircase. Liana crept up the stairs quietly and reached the top in little time.

Before her lay a large open room, the walls of which were lined with computers. Scattered across the room were bookshelves of varying heights. The room was unoccupied, just as Liana had expected, as most everyone had made their way to the training grounds. She quickly crossed the space to a large, tall, bookshelf that stood at the back of the room. Grabbing a chair, she pulled it across the room to the bookshelf. When she swiped her hand across the top, she knocked something to the floor.

Liana jumped down from the chair excitedly and pushed back the chair to the desk it had previously sat at before she ran over to grab the book that she had knocked off the shelf. It was pocket-sized and looked to be falling apart. The cover was a dull gray and appeared to have been through some things; the book was covered in several stains that Liana didn't care to know what from, and the pages seemed to be barely bound in the book.

After a moment of looking it over, Liana's sense of urgency overpowered her curiosity, and she quickly crossed the room. She headed back down the spiral staircase, and as her foot hit the landing of the hallway, she knocked into something.

"Liana! You aren't at the training grounds?" a surprised Nicolai exclaimed while he stood in front of her.

"Nicolai!" she shouted in a half-startled, half-excited to see him tone.

She quickly moved to hide the book from his view.

"Shouldn't *you* be at the training grounds?" she asked in a prying tone.

"Uhh, ya! I was looking for you, of course," he retorted, and rubbed the back of his neck with one hand. "Come on, let's go," he said while he put a hand on her shoulder and guided her toward the staircase.

Slowly, she tucked the book into the back of her shorts and covered it with her shirt. They made their way out of the back of the house and walked along the dirt path. They were making quick time coming up to the training grounds, and Liana knew she had to get rid of the book somehow. The forest was dense along the path that they walked; branches hung low stretching across the small dirt road. Liana saw the perfect opportunity and tripped over a small root that had surfaced in the path.

As she stumbled, she was able to toss the book into a nearby thicket, as Nicolai moved to help her to her feet. As they approached the training area, they quietly joined everyone who was gathered in the middle. Everyone stood in a circle around the trainer who stopped speaking as he saw Liana and Nicolai approach.

"Couldn't bother to be on time again?" he asked in a harsh tone.

Liana stood with her mouth slightly open, unable to come up with a good explanation.

"My apologies, Antonio. See I -" Nicolai began but was quickly cut off by the instructor as he held up his hand.

Antonio cut in sharply, "I sincerely doubt this had anything to do with you, Nicolai. Liana, come here."

Liana reluctantly made her way through the others to stand in front of Antonio.

"Since you seem to think I am joking about being on time to training, maybe Khius can help you understand the importance," he said as he bowed slightly to her and gestured to Khius in the crowd.

He waved with his hand, and signaled for Khius to join them. Khius halfheartedly moved to stand next to the instructor with a remorseful look on his face.

"First to spar today will be our volunteers, Khius and Liana," Antonio said in a booming voice for all to hear. "Ready?"

"What? Wait!" Liana cried out desperately as Khius mouthed sorry and raised his fists in front of his face.

"Attempt to overpower your opponent," he said as he backed out of the middle of the circle to stand with the crowd. "Begin."

"This hardly seems fa-" Liana's plead cut off as she saw Khius lunge at her.

She jumped back quickly, but his pursuit was persistent.

*Come on*, Khius mouthed to her, his eyes wide while he insisted she put up a fight.

Liana recalled some of her earlier training with Antonio and raised her arms to defend herself. She took an immediate step toward Khius and lifted her leg, heel first, to kick at his side. Khius quickly hooked her leg in his arm and reeled her toward him.

As she hopped for balance, she strained against him in an attempt to free her leg, but it was no use. As Khius pulled her close, he wrapped a large arm under hers and around the back of her neck. She struggled to free herself as she heard his whisper in her ear.

"Did you get the book?" he said, barely audible under the shouts of everyone that watched.

She nodded her head against his arm before she dropped her weight to the ground, freed herself from his grasp, and rolled a short distance. Now in a squatting position, Liana used this opportunity to kick Khius' legs from underneath himself. He tripped and stumbled backward, before he landed awkwardly on the ground. Liana got to her feet quickly and kicked Khius square in the shoulder, which sent him the rest of the way to the ground. She took the opportunity to pin him by placing her knees on his shoulders quickly.

"Hell ya!" Khius shouted with a wink to Liana.

Her cheeks flushed as she shook her head with a grin on her face at Khius' remarks.

She mouthed the word, *sorry*.

Liana raised a fist above him and was able to get a hit to his cheek before he bucked her off and sent her behind him. She landed on her hands and knees with Khius quickly to his feet behind her. His arm slid around her neck this time, and fear set in as his chokehold on her tightened. Her focus fell on Antonio, who stood in front of her, arms crossed over his chest. He wore a smug grin on his face and patiently waited for her defeat.

With a swift movement, Liana threw her weight against Khius' chest, knocking him backward on the ground. His grip on her did not break as she hoped it would, instead he pulled Liana down with him, and landed her on his chest. Frustration built in her as she started to realize she would not be able to win. Her supply of oxygen depleted as she grunted and struggled harder against Khius. Her hands gripped and dug into his massive arms, and attempted to pull them from her neck as a small shock emitted from her fingertips into Khius' skin.

"Hey! That's not fair!" he shouted in a fit of pain laced anger as he released her.

Confused at what just happened, she gasped for air she rolled off him to the ground while she tried to climb to her feet. As she stood, the room spun around her, and she stumbled. Khius was quick to his feet. He turned and kicked Liana square in the back. Khius climbed on top of her this time and rolled her to face him.

He mouthed, *sorry,* with a genuine look on his face as he raised a fist above her.

She couldn't move, her arms were pinned under his solid frame. Khius took a breath in and let his fist drop.

"Enough!" Antonio's voice cut sharply through the air.

Liana opened her eyes to see Khius' fist so close that her eyelashes brushed his skin. Khius quickly got to his feet and offered a hand to Liana. She took his hand gratefully before he yanked her to a standing position. He hugged her in a tight grip with a smile on her face.

"Not bad!" Khius said as everyone around them laughed and clapped enthusiastically.

"Correct, Khius. Not bad, terrible." Antonio said while he pushed between the two in the middle and turned to face the group that surrounded them. "When you're late," he shouted as he turned, and looked at each face in the crowd before he fixated on Liana, "you miss out on key practices that prove useful in these instances. THIS is the difference between winning and losing, between living and dying."

He paused for a moment, then turned, and walked out of the circle as he added, "Training is canceled. You cannot absorb a message you do not understand." Antonio lowered his head and walked away from the group, before he disappeared into the forest.

Nicolai stepped out of the crowd in front of Khius, face red with frustration while he questioned, "Do you understand the danger you're putting her in?"

"What are you talking about? We're all trying to keep her *out* of danger," Khius said as he looked around, and gestured to everyone.

Nicolai stood quietly and stared directly at Khius without blinking. After a tense moment of silence, he turned on his heel and pushed his way through the crowd. They all stood there, and watched Nicolai as he stomped off into the distance.

Everyone looked at each other in silence. Liana rubbed the back of her neck and kept her eyes on the ground awkwardly. Tension resonated in the air until, to Liana's surprise, Khius grabbed her at the waist and lifted her to his shoulder.

"Liana saved us from training!" Khius shouted at the crowd, to which the group retorted with a roar.

Liana exhaled a sigh of relief, followed by laughter. After a bit more cheering, Khius finally let her gently down to the ground, and the group turned to head back to the house.

"Man, you sure can put up a fight," Khius said with a laugh as he ran to catch up with Liana, who was caught up in the group of celebrants on the path back to the house.

"And you sir, you can take a hit."

She laughed as she turned, and gingerly punched him on the shoulder.

"Ahhh! Owe you relentless monster! Enough is enough!" he cried out as he stopped and grabbed at his shoulder while he faked an intense pain briefly, before he jogged to catch up to her since she hadn't stopped to pity him.

"I see you have some shocking talents on your hands," Khius said while he gestured to her hands.

"That came from me?" she asked and looked down at her hands.

He grinned and pulled her in for a quick side hug before he quietly said, "Only a glimpse of your power."

"Hey, I could sure use a drink after *not winning* like that." Liana said as she imitated Antonio's voice briefly before she cracked up with laughter.

The group who walked with her responded with a laugh, except Khius, whose face lit up as he stopped dead in his tracks.

"What?" she inquired while she stopped, and looked over Khius' face.

"I think we deserve to have ourselves a little party," he said in a hushed tone to the few that had gathered around as he rubbed his hands together in a scheming fashion.

"Not sure Nicolai'd like that too much," said a taller, ginger-haired man that stood next to Liana.

"Come on, Wes, I'm sure Khius has something up his sleeve," Liana said as she turned to Khius with an inquisitive look on her face.

She was hoping he'd take the bait and provide her a chance to slip away to retrieve the book she'd stashed. Also, she could really use a chance to chill out for once after weeks of intensive training. A grin spread across Khius' face as he began to unravel his plan.

# Chapter 11
## *The Book*

A knock sounded at Liana's bedroom door.

"What?" she yelled over the screams that sounded from her headset as her character on the game she played took a shot to the head.

The knock now grew to a loud bang on her door. She sighed, pulled her headset down around her neck, and heaved herself out of her bed.

"What!?" she yelled in an irritated tone as she wrenched open the door.

Rhythmic, music bumped from downstairs could be heard very clearly now that the door stood open.

"Sorry, couldn't hear you over the racket."

Wes beamed at her from the hall. His tall, slender form leaned against the wall waiting for Liana to answer.

"Come on! Nicolai is on a wild goose chase looking for me. He'll be gone for hours!" he said as he shoved a drink into Liana's hands and turned to head downstairs.

"We have a code P everyone!" she yelled into her headset before she threw it onto her bed and headed down the hall.

She was soon joined by a few more individuals, including Arietta, who joined arms with Liana. Weeks of long training and no fun at all had left everyone a little on edge, they were all glad to catch a break. They made their way downstairs to a room across from the dining area. It was already packed with people that danced to the beats that a DJ kept going. Liana broke free from Arietta and sat on a cushioned chair in the corner. She watched as Arietta joined Wes on the dance floor.

After a few drinks, Liana still couldn't help but think of the book she had stashed earlier that day. With everyone getting well into the festivities, she figured this was the perfect time to slip away. She got up and made her way across the open foyer. As she looked back to see if anyone took notice, she collided with the solid form of Khius.

"Whoa there, sneaky! Where you off to?" Khius laughed as he placed another drink in her hands.

"I'm good," she said as she smiled up at him and pushed it back. "Running to the restroom real quick," she said with a wink to him.

"Ahhh, gotcha!" he said rather loudly as he looked around.

Mouth half open in amazement at him, she squinted a look of frustration in his direction. She motioned her hands downward and implied for him to keep it down. Khius snorted out a laugh and put a finger over his lips as tiptoed in an exaggerated sense backward away from her.

Liana made her way out of the house with no further interruptions. A chilly breeze blew across her face as she stepped out into the night. Once she was clear from the sight of the house, she turned on a small flashlight that she had stashed in her pocket and broke out in a jog toward the area where she had hidden the book. It didn't take long for her to find it. Dusting off the small book, she noticed a set of tiny, strange, silver symbols on the cover. She didn't know what language it was, yet it seemed recognizable.

She eagerly placed the flashlight between her shoulder and cheek while she aimed it at the book. As she held the book in her hands, she noticed the symbols began to fade and shimmer like they shook on the page. Blinking rapidly, she looked around in the night's darkness, then back at the cover. The symbols were gone, replaced by scripted wording that read: *The Kingdom.*

The pages were all stuck together which caused the book to fall open to a section in the middle as Liana tried to open it. She skimmed through the text and tried to see what the book was all about. It spoke of a young Queen whose powers had to be taken from her when she was sentenced to be banished from her Kingdom. Careful not to damage the book, she gingerly unstuck a few pages to flip backward. Liana read that the Queen led an army of thousands into battle and sacrificed them to cover up a secret affair she had with the king of another nation.

Even though Liana felt terrible for this ordeal, she didn't understand what was so important about all of it. She flipped backward again in the book and opened it to a page where the title of the chapter showed a name. The crunching of twigs sounded rhythmically in the distance. Liana hurriedly stashed the book back in the bush and covered it with some leaves. When she stood and turned, she saw Nicolai as he strolled up the path.

"Oh, hey!" he said when he caught sight of Liana and brushed himself off.

"Nicolai?" she asked, barely audible through her hoarse voice. She cleared her throat before she continued in a casual tone, "What are you doing all the way out here?"

"I'm guessing no one wanted me at the party," he said bluntly.

"Oh… uh," she mumbled, at a loss for words.

"It's okay, really. I get it. I've been a bit uptight lately," he said while he scratched the back of his head and eyed the ground.

"A bit?" she said with a laugh as she walked past him toward the house.

"It's just..." He stopped her and grabbed her gently by the arm before he quietly continued, "I just worry about your safety."

She smiled at him while she said, "I'm a big girl Nic, promise."

"I know you are. You don't get it," he said as he raised a hand to her face and leaned in.

"Look," she said as she pulled away from him, and turned her face on the ground. "I -" she paused, "I can't, just wouldn't be right to-"

"I understand," Nicolai interrupted. "Really," he said as he walked past her. "Go on. I'm sure everyone's missing you at the party."

"What about you?"

"I'll be fine," he said with a laugh, "honestly."

Liana turned away from him slowly and walked back to the house. Her pace quickened as the sounds of the others grew in the distance. Once inside the house, she quickly made her way through the crowd and found Khius on a couch in the corner by himself.

"Just couldn't stay away?" he asked in a smug tone.

"Op, you caught me," she said, sarcasm thick in her voice.

Liana paused for a moment and looked at Khius with a funny look on her face.

"What?" he asked.

"Nothing… déjà vu or something," she said with a shrug and laughed it off awkwardly.

"Well?" he asked while he handed her a drink.

"I don't get it," she said as she plopped down on the cushion and took the drink from him.

"It's about you, dummy," he said with a laugh and gave her a friendly shove.

"What?"

"The book. It's about you."

"Oh..."

She was thinking about Nicolai, but her attention quickly shifted to the conversation with Khius. Looking off toward the wall, she tried to remember the details of the book.

"Wait… I killed… all those people."

A look of dread spread over her face.

"Hey," he said in a serious tone as he placed a hand on her shoulder, "it could've happened to any of us."

"What do you mean?"

"You weren't ready to have that kind of power. You gained it quickly, and no one taught you how to use it properly. You bet I would've blown up long before you did."

He gave a short, reassuring laugh.

"Yea, you know that's right!" she said loudly while she laughed at him, and tried to hide the guilt that grew on her face. "Still," she mumbled and looked down at her hands.

"Seriously, don't beat yourself up. I can help you, you know?"

"Really?"

"Yea! We've all been at this a while now. You're just getting your powers back. You don't want to blow up again." He leaned in and quietly added, "I swear that's what Nicolai's after."

"What do you mean?" she asked and looked at him, disbelief on her face.

Khius leaned in and spoke in a low voice, "Well, he was pissed when the council banished you. Said it wasn't your fault, but they weren't hearing any of it. He wants revenge; to get rid of them and start over with you."

"That's crazy!" she yelled while she leaned away from him and eyed him suspiciously.

He put a finger to his lips and leaned in again while he whispered, "Hey, be careful, you never know who's listening." He paused for a moment and glanced around before he continued in a quiet rushed tone, "Look, when I found out he was coming here, a bunch of us were all on board for bringing you back. They had no right to banish you for sure, but people talk, and I don't know who we can trust."

"Did he tell you that's what he wants to do?"

"Well, no, he's not exactly keen on sharing info, you know?"

She nodded.

"Just be careful... okay?" he said under his breath as he looked around.

"Yea... you too."

Liana sat back against the arm of the couch. Her thoughts weighed on her as the music thumped and boomed on. Khius sat up and squeezed her knee.

"Want anything?" he asked as he got to his feet.

She shook her head as she stared at her feet. He turned and walked off into the crowd.

"Woah, what's wrong with you?" Arietta questioned loudly as she approached Liana.

Liana cleared her throat and quickly got to her feet.

"Hey!" she exclaimed in an enthusiastic tone.

"No drink?"

"Nah… I think I'm gonna turn in for the night."

Liana moved cautiously between the couch and table that sat in front of it.

"What!" Arietta shouted at Liana while she got closer to her as though she was personally offended.

She shrugged in response and added, "Just have a lot on my mind."

Arietta leaned in close to Liana and used her free hand to pull Liana's hip close to her own.

Her breath swept playfully across Liana's neck as she whispered, "Only trust yourself."

Liana jerked back and eyed her suspiciously.

"I said," Arietta thundered while her eyes darted about, "Do you want a shot, or do you really want to have a lot on your mind?"

Liana stared at her for a minute, absolutely confused.

"A… shot…" she said slowly while she tried to figure out if she had misheard Arietta.

Arietta winked at her.

"Get this woman a shot! Pronto!" she yelled as she pulled Liana through the crowd to a small bar set up along the back wall.

Arietta's outburst had drawn the attention of many of the other party-goers. Round after round was poured as everyone knocked back several drinks. Every time Liana stood to leave, Arietta would grab her arm and pour another shot.

After what seemed like hours, Liana was quite unsure how she was still functioning. Person after person tapped out and left the room in a drunken stumble before they retreated to their own room, but Liana and Arietta persevered. Late into the night, the music stopped, and the crowd dwindled to just the two of them. Arietta reached behind the bar for yet another bottle.

"I honestly should be getting to bed," Liana said as she stood in an attempt to leave again.

"We're finally alone," Arietta pleaded, "Now we can actually have a drink and talk."

"*Actually* have a drink?" Liana laughed with her words, "We've been drinking the whole time!"

Liana dropped her head and looked at Arietta as though she were insane. Arietta laughed as she poured two shots, stood, and handed one to Liana.

"Take a few of these and then tell me we've been drinking the whole time."

"Wait…"

Liana paused to take a shot. The bitter liquid burned on the way down while she squinted in response.

"We haven't been drinking? How was everyone getting so drunk?"

"Well, we've been drinking, but…" Arietta paused, raised her hand, and wiggled her fingers before she continued, "We haven't really been drinking."

Liana rolled her eyes, sat beside Arietta, and poured two more shots while she mumbled, "Everyone loves to speak riddles around here."

Arietta laughed as she clinked her glass against Liana's and downed it.

"I can purify your blood and remove the alcohol through skin to skin contact," she said nonchalantly as though she discussed her ability to breath. "How do you think you lasted this long?"

Liana busted out in laughter as she knocked back her glass and replied, "I honestly thought I was *that* awesome."

"Well, I mean..." she poured another shot for each of them and drank hers before she continued, "You did last a while. Really surprised me, but I kept you going."

She winked at Liana. Liana downed another shot, and the warm liquid began to take its grip on her.

"Okay, I think I'm getting there, now that you stopped cheating," she said with a light laugh.

Arietta laughed and leaned her chin against her hand as she leaned on the bar and gazed at Liana.

"Look," she started slowly, "I'm not trying to add to the chaos in your head." She paused and looked down at the bar before she continued, "I can't imagine what you're going through right now."

"Yea, no joke," Liana said as she sat back in her stool and looked at Arietta.

"Just..." She hesitated a moment and glanced around before she spoke in a quiet tone, "Just be careful putting much of any trust in anyone right now."

Liana nodded.

"Come on." Arietta poured another shot each before she added, "One for the road."

With a laugh, Arietta handed Liana the drink. Liana jumped down from her stool and took the glass. They clinked them together again, stared at each other for a moment, then downed the shots. Arietta walked with her back to her room and embraced her at her door. Liana felt her drunkenness as it slowly slipped away.

"Hey!" Liana said while she pushed Arietta off her and scolded, "Maybe I want to be drunk!"

Arietta laughed while she jumped back and countered, "Hey, gotta keep your wits about you."

Liana rolled her eyes, backed into her room, and with a grin, slammed her door.

"I'm down the hall if you need me," Arietta sang playfully through the door.

"Yea, yea," she said in response as she crossed her room to the balcony.

She threw open the curtains and opened the door beyond it, letting the warm night's breeze drift across her room. As she made her way back across the room to her bed, she slowly dropped her clothes along the way. The silky sheets felt cool on her skin as she climbed into the soft, comforting bed. Scents of lavender relaxed her as she pressed her face into her pillow and let out a brief frustrated scream.

How could she be so surrounded, yet so alone? She didn't even know who to trust anymore. Thoughts in her head urged her to make a run for it. Yet, at the same time, pushed her to stand and fight. A war was waged in her head, and there wasn't a clear side for her to choose. Her longing for the comforting days of a cubicle and wagging tail clawed up inside her again. She felt an undeniable pull that she was being guided here for a reason. If she could keep going, she wanted to believe everything would work out for the best.

*What if it didn't,* she asked herself and stared at the distant wall as a tear rolled down her cheek. *What if this is all for nothing?* She took a long deep breath and squeezed her eyes shut.

Deep inside, a reassuring voice echoed in her mind, though it didn't sound like hers, *All things are working for the best, but how will you know unless you keep fighting?*

A long exhale escaped her lips as the late night's breeze drifted over her bare back with a comfort that lulled her into a deep sleep.

○ ○ ○

With a sharp inward breath, Liana woke suddenly. She sat straight up in her bed and gripped the blankets to her chest as she glanced around the room. After a moment, she took a deep breath and shook her head before she rubbed her pulsing temples that screamed out at the light that so intrusively invaded her room. Annoyed grumbles escaped her tired form as she got to her feet. Liana made her way to the restroom and splashed her face with water before she pulled on a pair of sweatpants and a white tank top.

She made her way slowly down the stairs and crept toward the kitchen. Liana made it there in silence and happily poured herself a large glass of tomato juice. The cold, salty, liquid poured down her throat and disappeared in one drink. She could feel the creeping headache recede as she rinsed the glass in the sink and turned to make her way back upstairs.

Her hand slid up the door leading to the dining room, pushed it open, and lingered in the air above her head as she let out a tiny squeal with her stretch. She heard someone clear their throat as she stood there, mid-stretch, arms still in the air and looked out over the full dining room of numerous faces that all stared back at her in silence.

"Now that sleeping beauty is present," Arietta laughed, "everyone ready to get started?"

The group nodded to Arietta as they stood in unison and cleared their plates from the table. As they all hustled about Liana, she stood in confusion.

"What are we getting started?" she asked Nicolai in a confused tone as he passed by her.

"We're not seriously stopping training because Antonio threw a fit. We had plenty of other fun stuff planned anyway!" he explained while he smiled at her, an amused look on his face as the others gave a good laugh at the idea.

"Nooo," she dropped her head back in a whiney, childish manner.

It seemed her plans of sleeping the day away would be thwarted by Nicolai's obsession with perfection. She grumpily fell in with the rest of the group. Arietta tossed her a muffin while they finished cleaning the breakfast Liana missed out on. Liana gave a quick smile and nod of thanks before she devoured it and joined everyone as they grouped in the foyer.

"Alright," Khius began in an overly excited tone, "this *will* be a timed challenge."

Khius looked right at Liana as if this were the news to make her day.

"The goal is to get Liana out as quickly as possible. Preferably, with as many of us as possible," Khius quickly explained.

They passed around a box of noise-canceling headphones as he spoke.

"Great," Liana sighed under her breath as the box made it to her.

She really hoped the maze was a one-time event, and she'd never have to see it again.

"Ready, everyone?" Khius stood with his wrist held out, ready to hit the button on his watch.

"Wait, don't we need to head to the maze first?" Liana looked around at everyone, confused while she asked, "No blindfolds this time?"

Khius rolled his eyes, ignored her questions, and shouted, "Go!"

As he pressed the button on his watch, everyone slid the headphones over their ears. Liana followed suit as she looked around. Khius stepped to the side to reveal a small closet door under the foyer stairs. With a yank, he opened the door and revealed a tiny room. Khius kicked back a rug to reveal a trap door and quickly made his way down the ladder with a grin and a thumbs up to everyone before his head disappeared.

One by one, they all followed behind him quickly. Liana dropped her head to the left and right while she stretched the stiffness in her neck out. She raised her arms and twisted to the side as Arietta placed a hand on her back and gave her a friendly nudge toward the door. The echo of her sigh reverberated against the headphones and back into her head. She rolled her eyes, annoyed at her own attitude, and quickly started down the ladder. Only a few rungs down and her feet began to ache from the slender metal rungs that dug in at every step. As she looked around her, she wondered how much further they had to go and quickly understood why they weren't wearing blindfolds.

She turned her attention back to the rungs and concentrated while she descended as quickly as possible into the engulfing darkness. With every step, the small amount of light above her diminished until suddenly it was gone. The ladder vibrated slightly in her grasp, and she realized why the light above her was cut off. The vibrations on the ladder became more intense as someone came down above her, and Liana's picked up her pace.

The cold stone floor reached up to meet her feet as Liana reached the end of the ladder. With a grateful breath she backed away and into the chest of someone. She turned to the person she bumped into and let her hand travel up their solid torso to their shoulder. Liana stepped around the person to stand behind them and, in doing so, caught the scent of Nicolai. She lingered close to him and rested her head on her hand for a moment.

A welcome breeze from someone as they walked by brought the smell of pine and cedar to Liana again. She closed her eyes in the darkness while comfort crept up in her from the familiarity of his scent until she thought how strange it would look if anyone else could see her. Liana cleared her throat and stood up straight, while she shook her head and prepared herself for the task at hand. She could feel Nicolai begin to walk as his shoulder moved from her grasp. Quickly, she reached out, and grabbed his shoulder tight, nervous about losing him again in the darkness. Her grip tightened further as the group's pace quickened.

*Khius is really serious about timed training,* she thought to herself as she let out a laugh.

She felt Nicolai's hand wander up her fingertips that she noticed were dug into his shoulder. He gave her hand a squeeze, and she immediately let up on her grip. So focused on keeping up, she hadn't noticed the death grip she had on Nicolai. His warm, steady hand lingered a moment after her grip let up before he suddenly jerked it away.

Several twists and turns later, they came to a sudden stop. Liana impatiently rocked back and forth on her aching bare feet as the icy grips of the stone floor set in. Liana groaned as time appeared to stand still. Another annoying sigh reverberated back in Liana's ears, accompanied by an unseen eye roll directed at her annoyance with herself.

Irritation set in under her skin as time continued to pass with no signs of the group moving on. She couldn't take the waiting any longer. Her hand left Nicolai's shoulder, traveled down his bicep and to his hand that rested on another individual's shoulder. As she walked on, she was reminded of the grip on her shoulder. With her free hand, she reached up to the hand on her shoulder. After just a moment, they released her. She placed their hand on Nicolai's shoulder before she continued up the line. Her hand traveled along shoulders and down arms until she reached the front.

Her free hand grasped in front of her into the darkness in an attempt to interpret her surroundings. Like a moth to the flame, her hand immediately met with the face of someone in front of her. Liana cringed as her hand ran over the tightly cropped, coarse hair of Khius. Her hand traveled down the back of his head to his neck, where she gave him a light pat in the attempt to say, *sorry*.

Khius reached up, gripped her wrist in his massive hand and gave her arm a sudden yank forward. Liana involuntarily released the shoulder of the person she previously anchored herself to and found herself standing next to Khius. He pulled her wrist, and guided her hand to a cold, solid metal surface. She stepped forward and freed her wrist from his grip.

Her hands journeyed all over the metal surface until they discovered a round wheel. Excitement crossed her face as she gripped on to the wheel and tried to turn it.

With all her strength, to no avail, she attempted to turn the wheel in either direction. She dropped her head and shook it for a moment before she laughed at herself. Her hand reached out behind her in the darkness and searched for Khius. After a few seconds of grabbing at thin air, she began to flail her arm back and forth.

Liana cringed again as her wrist connected with the strong cheekbone of Khius' face. She rubbed it for a moment before his hand grabbed her wrist to yank it away. Liana pulled her wrist back from his grip and grabbed Khius' arm that gripped hers. He released her wrist and allowed her to feel around for the door again. After a moment of awkward groping on the door, she found the wheel and placed Khius' hand on it. She released his hand and gave it a pat as she attempted to urge him to try.

He reached back out for her and grabbed her arm. Khius put Liana's palm face-up on his own and began to touch the center of her palm with a series of taps as if trying to communicate with Morse code. He then placed her hand on the door again. She had no clue what he was trying to say or what he wanted her to do.

While she felt around the door again, she searched for anything that could help. After a few frustrating moments, her hand slid over something rough and bumpy. Her heart skipped a beat as she backtracked and searched for whatever it was she just felt. Suddenly her hand glided over it again. She felt over the rough bumps. They were several small, square, rubber, buttons in a larger square shape. Suddenly it hit her.

"A keypad!" she shouted out for no one to hear.

As she turned back to Khius with excitement, she reached out again and tensed for the moment she'd punch him in the face for the third time. His hand gripped her wrist out of nowhere. A smile spread on her face as she pulled his hand to the keypad. Khius instantly nudged her to the side, away from the door. She waited a few moments before a blinding light met her eyes.

"Ugh!" she cried out in pain as her hands found her eyes while she simultaneously turned around and doubled over.

"Sorry!" she heard from Khius as he pulled her noise-canceling headphones off and handed them back to her.

She turned to him, grabbed the headphones, and shrugged, "Sorry for punching you… a lot."

They laughed as the others filed out of the dark into a bright open field. She looked back to see a large vault door with the dark hallway they had come from that stood in the side of a hill hidden under tall grass and shrouded by large shrubs.

"Ten minutes! Not bad, but I think we could do better," Khius shouted over everyone who carried on in conversation with one another.

"Ten minutes? It felt like an eternity!" Liana said in disbelief.

"That's because Khius can't unlock a freakin' door," Arietta teased from the door as she latched it shut and walked toward Liana.

"Hey! That lock is in a terrible place," Khius said defensively.

"I didn't have any problems finding it," Liana said with a shrug as she walked off toward Nicolai, who was with a group of the others heading back to the house.

"Yea… well…" Khius trailed off as he realized no one listened to him.

Arietta laughed before she punched Khius in the arm.

"Takes a team, man," she said to him as she jogged to catch up to Liana.

# Chapter 12
## *The King*

Liana woke with a start to the sounds of shouts. She instantly sat up and saw several women that scrambled around her room; only it didn't seem like her room. The room felt memorable, but it didn't look like any place she'd been before. The bedroom walls seemed to be made from a marble-like material and faded as she tried to focus on them.

A woman that ran about suddenly came to Liana, grabbed her arm, and pulled her from the bed. Their faces were blurry and unrecognizable, but they felt familiar. Though they moved about her with speed, Liana didn't feel panicked or rushed. They all pulled and tugged at her, at her hair, at her clothes.

Elated laughter sounded distantly from the hall as the ladies redressed her and weaved flowers into her hair. She wore a simple white lace and silk dress; it rested at the edge of her shoulders and fell to her knees. Liana suddenly noticed a woman stood still before her. She appeared to speak but Liana only caught fragments of what the woman said.

"Smile… intelligence… pay attention!"

The words echoed in and out as though they danced about the room playfully, but Liana definitely caught the end. She snapped to it in time to meet the woman's scrutinizing gaze with an innocent smile.

"That's it!" another woman said as she smacked Liana on the cheeks.

Liana blinked several times while her hand rose to her cheek. She began to realize she was in a dream but was confused but the tinge of pain that felt all too real. Liana looked up and tried to focus on the events around her. The women all giggled excitedly around her, except the one that stood in front of her. She suddenly reached down and seized Liana in a firm grip.

Quickly and silently, she guided her through a series of dark halls to a large foyer and out to a path. As she followed the path with her eyes, she saw it led to a white and gold stone street. Liana felt a bit of unease as the woman released her, and she began to walk down the path. This looked like no town Liana knew of. Large trees with golden bark lined the street in every direction, all stood broad in full bloom with tiny colorful blossoms.

In contrast to the house, everything appeared so bright outside, as if light radiated from every object. Large open buildings of white and gold smooth stone were stacked high around the streets with trees that wove through their structures. Golden vines traced the smooth curves and arches of the buildings, accenting their beauty. Throngs of people clothed in long, golden garments lined the streets, the middle of which numerous women walked, all dressed similar to Liana.

As she reached the street, she hesitated, and stepped part of the way from the path. When she stopped to observe everything around her for only a moment, the crowd began to fade. Liana panicked and hurriedly moved to step into the road but tripped as she left the path and stumbled awkwardly into the street. Embarrassed, she cleared her throat, then noticed she held the attention of a woman she nearly bumped into, who smiled and gestured for her to follow.

Liana absently followed the crowd of women in the street as she took in the scenery around her. As they rounded a curve, a towering castle came into view. Golden vines trailed up tall white pillars that held large open balconies of white and gold stone. The large white and golden walls of the castle were periodically accented by floor to ceiling, golden stained windows. Trees full of large white blossoms grew throughout the castle, and periodically showed through a window or roof section.

The women all stopped in a courtyard in front of the castle. They chattered amongst themselves excitedly. Liana remained silent while she looked around curiously. A hush came over the crowd as a man came out from the castle doors.

A crown of golden vines adorned his long, white-blonde hair that fell to his lower back over white and gold silk robes, which accented his golden-olive skin perfectly. His slender face and strong jaw were free from any imperfections. A golden glow seemed to emit from around him as he walked with a slow movement that drew in the crowd. He didn't speak to them, only looked out on the people with a tired, distant look on his face. Only a moment passed before he turned and walked back into the castle.

"Well, that was exciting," she said in a hushed, sarcastic voice aloud to herself.

A young woman by Liana's side, about Liana's age and height, with silky, dark mocha skin and tightly curled hair, giggled. She looked at Liana and gave her a thumbs up. Liana looked at the girl quizzically, then turned her attention back to the castle. After a short time, another man came from the same entrance and spoke to guards in a hushed tone.

Complete silence fell over the crowd as the guards walked from the castle, through the group of women. They tapped a few of the women's shoulders as they passed by them, and the corresponding women made their way to the stairs, where they waited. When the guards made their way past Liana, they tapped her and the girl to her side. The girl let out a small squeal, grabbed Liana's wrist, and practically hauled her up to the stairs at the castle's entrance.

Liana turned and looked out over the crowd. Their faces were all a blur, except one. In the distance, she could've sworn she saw Nicolai. A golden hood was drawn up over his hair, and blocked most of his face from the light. Their eyes connected as the girl next to Liana gave her a tug. When she turned to look back at the crowd, he was no longer there.

The guards made their way back through the crowd and escorted the women into the castle. Liana followed the group through a set of large wooden doors with intricate golden details laid in them. The doors opened to an extensive entrance hall that housed a massive tree in the middle, the trunk of which Liana was sure the whole group could fit into. The fragrance of it filled the air with a sweet, honey-like smell. Liana felt herself relax as she inhaled deeply.

They walked through the foyer, around the tree, and to a hallway off to her right. The corridor, though narrow, had high vaulted ceilings with windows along the walls near the ceiling, which allowed their path to be bright and feel open. They were led along the hallway to a large open room with glass windows for walls and large pillars that periodically reached high up to the ceiling. Altogether there were a dozen women that entered the hall. Liana was at the end; she straggled behind as she looked around and gawked at the grandeur of the marvelous castle.

The man who previously appeared to the crowd now sat on a golden, granite throne. His prominent temple was adorned by a golden crown that curved elegantly around his sapphire eyes. He looked strong and stern but had a bored demeanor. He leaned with his chin in his palm that he propped up on the arm of the throne. He glanced up periodically as the women filed in, that was until his eyes fell on Liana.

She glanced down shyly, but she could tell he still looked at her, as though he studied her. His posture straightened as she neared, and his expression shifted to one of curiosity. A dark, muscular man with a chiseled chin and bright blue eyes sat to his right. He leaned in as the King whispered to him, and their eyes never fell from Liana.

Unexpectedly, a towering guard appeared at her side. The guard guided her by the elbow from the other women before they reached the King. The guard led her past white marble pillars down a hall to the left of the King's throne. She looked back to the other women whose blurred faces were bent towards each other while they whispered excitedly. The guard escorted her down a long corridor to a large white door.

He opened it and motioned for her to go inside. As she entered the room, the guard shut the door behind her. Turning anxiously, she noticed there was just a wall where the door once stood. Liana took a deep breath, trying to remind herself this was all a dream as she turned to look around her. The simple large room was bare except for a decorative bench in the middle.

After a moment, she walked over to it. She ran her hand over the dark, carved decorations in the wood, then along the soft, white, velvety material. She turned and sat slowly on the bench while she looked around the vaulted room. Before long, she heard a click from a door as it appeared in front of her. The door slowly opened as the King she had previously seen entered. She stood as he walked toward her and kept her eyes on the floor, but the room began to fade away.

Before she knew it, she saw the white canopy of the bed she had fallen asleep in. Rolling over, she quickly pulled her pillow over her head and tried to submerge back in her dream or at least remember every little detail. A warm breeze blew through the open doors of her balcony and brought the blinding light with it as it ruffled the curtains. Liana groaned as she knew it was doubtful she'd be going back to sleep.

○ ○ ○

Various grunts and groans sounded from around the vast training grounds as Liana made her way around the obstacles. She paused a moment when she reached the center open area where Khius sparred with a cunning Wes. After a few laughs at Wes' speed overcoming Khius, she set off to the farthest side of the training grounds where Arietta stood, arms crossed, and waited.

As Liana approached, Arietta shouted, "Let's go sunshine!"

Liana rolled her eyes as she picked up her pace and let a grin spread across her face. After a short distance, Liana came to a stop in front of Arietta and looked around.

"I'm afraid to ask what the plan is," she said with a nervous laugh.

Arietta's huge, childlike grin was almost infectious until Liana followed the pointing finger of Arietta's, up to a rope that hung several feet above the both of them.

"Uh..."

Liana rubbed the back of her neck as she took a step back and allowed her eyes to follow the rope several more feet in the air to the spidering canopy of ropes that intertwined above them.

"Nah, nope… pass. Sorry. Don't think so," Liana said as she shrugged at Arietta.

Arietta crossed her arms over her chest and cocked her head to the side.

"At least give it a try. Like the dress. You didn't think that'd work, but it was awesome. This will be awesome!" she urged Liana.

"Hey, that dress go me drugged and kidnapped. Even more of a reason to say no to this," Liana waved her hand up at the ropes, "shenanigan."

Arietta almost looked offended as she took a few steps toward Liana and said, "Hey, don't blame that dress. They wanted you. You could've been wearing sweatpants, and they would've done the same thing!"

Liana nodded her head with her reply, "Okay, but still."

Liana looked up at the canopy of ropes.

"Everything looks intimidating at the start. Just jump and take it one part at a time. I'm right here. Let's go!" Arietta shouted while she jumped several times excitedly.

Liana couldn't help but grin as she let out a huge sigh and breathed, "Fine!"

She drew in a long breath as she stood before the rope and looked up at it while it hung just out of reach yet in her face. After only a moment, she drew in a sharp breath, squatted, then jumped and reached as high as she could. Her fingers brushed the bottom of the rope, and narrowly missed it. With a grumble, she stretched her legs out, then jumped again. This time her hand connected with the bottom of the rope, and she gripped on tight.

"Good! Good. Now pull yourself up," Arietta spoke calmly from below.

Liana's muscles already cried out in protest. She forced herself to focus on the rope as she reached up with her other hand and grabbed higher up. With a deep breath, she pulled herself up higher and higher on the rope. Soon she was able to grab the rope between her legs and feet.

"Keep moving," Arietta sounded from directly beneath her as Liana felt her slap the side of her shoe.

"What are you doing?!" Liana shouted down.

Arietta laughed with her reply, "Gotta keep you moving."

Liana reached up for the rope to continue, but her hand met air. Looking up, she noticed they had reached the intertwined canopy of ropes. She pulled herself up into a sitting position on top and rested while Arietta followed behind her. The breeze blew over the open canopy and across Liana's back. She closed her eyes, soaking in the gentle rays of sun that periodically peeked out from behind the clouds.

"It's so peaceful up here," Liana said while she looked at Arietta.

"Yea," Arietta said from a standing position on top of the ropes near Liana. "I love to come up here sometimes at night and look up at the stars."

Liana looked up as if she could see the stars herself.

"Let's get a move on," Arietta said as she turned to awkwardly navigate passed Liana on the ropes.

"Where are we going?" Liana asked, confused.

Arietta laughed. "We aren't just climbing a rope. We're going across."

Liana groaned.

"Come on, that was the hard part," she said as she gestured down to the rope they just climbed before she turned from Liana. "Any movement forward is better than sitting still," Arietta yelled over her shoulder.

Liana rolled her eyes as she awkwardly attempted to get to her feet. As she stood, the ropes moved and shook beneath her trembling legs. She nervously stooped to grab on to the ropes and began to crawl in Arietta's direction. With each step and unsure placement of her footing, she grew in confidence. Before long, she slowly walked.

"See, you got it!" Arietta shouted from a distance.

Liana looked up to see Arietta quite a distance away with a large hole between the two of them. She swayed as her confidence shook, and she stooped to sit on the ropes again.

"Just rest for a moment, then keep going. We're almost there," Arietta said as she bounced on the ropes.

Liana could feel the movements of Arietta vibrate through the ropes and jostle her as they reached her. Slowly, she got to her feet and made her way across the ropes. Liana examined the giant hole in the ropes canopy between Arietta and herself. She peeked down into the gap and noticed they were above the sparring ring. Quite a few feet below them, Khius and Wes could be seen still attempting to overpower one another. Liana gave a little chuckle.

"Watch this," she muttered to Arietta. "Khius!" she shouted suddenly.

Khius looked up instantly and grinned at Liana just before he took a shoulder to the chest, courtesy of Wes.

"Sorry!" Liana cringed.

Liana made her way around the opening in the ropes to join Arietta. Together, they gradually made their way across the canopy to the other side. Liana wiggled between an opening in the canopy where she saw a rope dangle.

"Just ease yourself down," Arietta said from behind her.

Liana gripped the rope between her shoes and slowly lowered herself away from the canopy. Only a few inches down the rope, her muscles burned and protested in exhaustion. She took a deep breath as she looked up. To her horror, she saw Arietta coming down right above her. She looked back at the rope in her hands and concentrated on lowering herself down it. In a rush, she lost her grip and began to slide down the rope. The harder she tried to grab on, the faster she slid.

"Let go!" Arietta shouted.

Liana let go just as she reached the edge of the rope, and her feet hit the ground. She looked up to Arietta, a sense of accomplishment on her face, and laughed as she brushed the loose hair from her eyes. Cringing, she looked down at her rope-burned hands, and shook them.

"Better than a broken neck," Arietta said while she shrugged before she nudged Liana's shoulder.

Liana nodded at her, as she said, "Quite."

Arietta walked off toward a path that led from the training grounds with her hand in the air and said, "You can go do whatever now. I'm done maiming you."

A chuckle could be heard from her beyond the trees as she disappeared into them.

# Chapter 13
## *Privacy*

Liana lay sprawled out on her bed, stomach full of dinner and legs aching from the training session with Arietta. She mindlessly flipped through the channels on the television across the room as the door to the left of it swung open without notice, and Khius' form pushed through.

"Hey, you have a sec?" he asked, but didn't wait for an answer before he moved to shut the door and come in.

"Sure. What's the point of those dogs anyway? They don't seem to keep *you* away," she said half playful, half too tired to deal with anyone as she threw the remote at him and sat up in bed.

He laughed and caught the remote, then turned the television up ridiculously loud. A knock sounded from the other side of her door.

"Geeze, everybody just come on over!" she groaned, irritated.

She could see it was Nicolai, but he didn't come in. He and Khius exchanged a few words which were drowned out by the television; then, he was gone. Khius kicked off his shoes and socks. He grabbed up one of his socks and threw it over the doorknob before he shut it and walked over to Liana.

"What the... What's going on?" she asked suspiciously, her voice raised over the incredibly loud racket that sounded from the T.V.

Khius walked around to the side of her bed.

"Oh, we won't have to worry about being disturbed if they think we're," he made a crude gesture in the air where he pulled his fists toward his groin, "ya know."

"Lovely," she said.

With the roll of her eyes, she scooted back in her bed, and allowed Khius room. He crawled clumsily across the blanket and sat across from Liana cross-legged.

"And the noise?" she asked, only half annoyed at this point.

"More privacy," he said with a smile.

"Right."

"Ready to get a grip on these powers?"

"Now? I'm a bit tired, honestly."

"Perfect!" he exclaimed as he reached up and grabbed her arms. "Show me that shocky thing again."

"I can't just do it. I said that was an accident, remember?"

"Can you do anything else?" he asked.

"I don't know."

"What do you mean you don't know?"

Her exhaustion brought with it a quick temper, and she snapped at him, "I said I don't know, okay!"

*Doesn't take much,* she heard a distant voice in her mind, *to set her off.*

She pulled her arms away and studied him. She could've sworn she heard him speak, but she didn't see his lips move.

"Were you talking…just now," she asked.

"We've been talking…"

"No, just now. You said it didn't take much to set me off."

Khius' eyes grew huge with excitement, and a look of surprise crossed his face.

"What! No way! You heard what I was thinking!" He paused for a moment in his celebration as a sly smile spread across his face and he said, "You heard what I was thinking."

"Yea..." Liana said while she eyed him suspiciously.

She thought back to her encounter with Khius when she first got to the house. Maybe she wasn't crazy after all.

"Awesome! Let's work on *that* power."

"Uhm, I think the shock thing would be better," he said while he pulled his once outstretched hands away from hers.

Laughing loudly, she asked, "You scared? I thought we were working on my *powers*, like multiple, not just *one*."

He glared at her with his reply, "Fine."

She reached up, grabbed his hands and with a bit of excitement, asked, "Okay, what do we do."

"Read my mind," he said in a smart-aleck tone.

"I don't know how I did it."

"A bit of a slow learner, I see," he said and grinned back at her.

"You're supposed to be helping me, not insulting me!" she retorted quickly while she grew increasingly aggravated.

*Come on, dumbass,* a voice not her own echoed loudly in her head. *Figure it out.*

Her face lit up and she exclaimed, "I heard that!"

"You look awfully excited for me just calling you a dumbass," he said before he laughed and pulled his hands back to his side. "Most of our powers are usually tied to our emotions. If you can control your emotions and focus on the power tied to them, you should be able to channel the power and control it."

Liana closed her eyes and attempted to concentrate on Khius irritating her while she tried to hear him, but after a long pause, she heard nothing. Khius reached up and grabbed her elbow.

Instantly, she heard him loud and clear, *We'll see if this works.*

"I did it again!" she cheered before she lunged at him and wrapped him in a tight hug.

He laughed awkwardly and embraced her for a moment before he pushed her back to her seat on the bed as he said, "Looks like you have to make contact. Think of it as my thoughts flowing through me to you."

"Got it. So… what about the shocking?"

"Well, since it's a different power, it's probably tied to a different emotion. Think about what you were thinking or feeling at that moment and focus on that. Once you know how they work, you can work on controlling them."

"What kind of stuff can you do?" she asked while she eyed him curiously.

"Hey, that's kind of personal," he said while he looked around awkwardly as if someone else listened.

"And this isn't?" she questioned while she motioned between them.

"You've already experienced one of my powers."

She looked at him, confused and asked, "What do you mean?"

He raised his hand to cover her eyes. She was instantly in another room. A man entered the door in front of her, with long blonde hair and a golden crown of vines that he wore with white and gold silk robes. Liana recognized him instantly.

He gave a smile while he quietly spoke, "She's out there, Khius."

"Should I go get her?" she asked in a voice that came from her but wasn't hers.

"Send the guards. Retrieve others along with her. I know she's the one," The King said before he embraced her and walked off behind her.

She walked toward the door and reached out with the strong hands of Khius as her own to open it. As the door opened, she could see a large crowd that expanded as far as she could see, each individual murmuring to one another. Instantly she could feel Khius' hand move from her face, and she opened her eyes. She saw she still sat in her room with Khius.

"That wasn't a dream," she mumbled to herself.

"No, that was my memory." He shrugged and continued, "Not quite as shocking as your powers, but it's handy."

"Can you show any memory?"

"I can show whatever I want." He sat back, crossed his arms across his chest and explained, "They don't even have to be memories. Nicolai begged me to warn you of the others trying to kidnap you. Remember your dreams before all of this?"

She looked down at her bedspread in thought for a moment before she suddenly asked, "Wait… you were in my room and my office?"

"No!" He laughed before he explained, "I can project it to you if I need to." He lifted his hands near her face and said, "This way is just easier. Doesn't take as much out of me."

"I'm going to keep my eye on you," she said while she narrowed her eyes at him and leaned away.

He laughed and said, "Don't worry. I'm on your side."

"Wait! You knew the King?" she asked excitedly.

He stood up from the bed and faced away from her before he replied in a quiet, somber tone, "He was my brother."

Intrigued, she sat there and stared at him. Though she wanted to ask him a million questions, she could tell this wasn't the time but didn't know what to say, so she sat in silence.

"Anyway," he said and suddenly snapped back to his usual self before he turned to face her. "Get some rest. The more you use your powers, the more they drain you."

He crossed the room in a few strides.

"Khius!" she yelled over the television's blare.

"Yea?" he asked, hand on the doorknob while his back remained to her.

"Thanks."

He paused and smiled at the door before he replied, "Go to sleep."

Liana collapsed backward on her feathered bedspread she was seated on and drifted into a deep slumber. Images swirled around her as she tried to focus. She was escorted into a simple vaulted room with white crystalline walls. The room was bare except for a decorative bench in the middle. Slowly, she approached the seat while she ran her hand over the dark wooden engravings and soft, white, plush material.

As she turned to sit on the bench, she noticed a door in front of her. Slowly she lowered herself and looked around the vaulted room. She tried to focus, to concentrate on something, anything. Her blurry hands ran along the white, lace dress she wore and could feel the rough and silky details of the gown. Though the harder she focused, the more everything seemed to slip away.

A loud click from the door in front of her drew her attention. She looked up to see the door slowly open. A tall man stepped through the door and stood still as it closed and clicked shut behind him. He was clad in white garments with golden trim and wore a crown of golden vines. His floor-length white and gold, royal mantle fell behind his shoulders, secured with an ornate, gold-brushed clasp at his collarbone. It all seemed so familiar to Liana, and suddenly she realized.

She focused and tried not to let the dream slip by her this time. Liana met the King's gaze and stood as he crossed the room to move around her. He stood there and looked over her for a moment as she studied his face. He put a hand beneath her chin and raised it to meet his gaze. Instantly she was lost in his eyes. There was no trying to focus for Liana. She could see every detail in his eyes clearly, a dark silver outline incased profound pools of sapphire that dove deeper than any ocean.

His muffled speech sounded around her, but she did not force herself to listen; only stood there and gazed into his eyes. He took her hand in his and motioned for her to follow. He turned to stand beside her for a moment before he led her out of the room and down a narrow hallway. They rounded the corner, where the walkway opened up to a balcony. Liana looked out over the balcony to find a crowd that cheered with excitement. She looked out over the many faces confused as she began to lose focus again. A muffled announcement was made that caused the crowd to cheer even louder.

As she turned to look to the man beside her, he placed on her head, a crown of intricately woven silver, adorned by stones that radiated light from within. He motioned for her to face the crowd and lifted her hand as she did. The crowd roared even louder. Liana slid from the crowd as she woke slowly. The images of the castle swirled in her head as she rubbed her eyes. Sitting up on her elbows, she thought for a few moments about the dreams that she had been having. She was quite certain some of them were memories that linked her back to a life she had been forced to forget, but she couldn't decipher what was what.

Gradually, she climbed out of her bed and walked to the balcony of her room, where she opened the curtains and stepped out into the cool morning air. The stars still shined in the early morning sky. While she looked up, she thought again about how much she missed her old life. She wondered about the office and longed for a chance to sit and watch the lightning bugs in the quiet of her old yard. It didn't seem fair that she was dragged into all this chaos. She wanted it to end, but still knew she had to keep going. It wasn't about her anymore.

As she shook her head, she thought, *That wasn't even your real life... this is.*

She examined the grounds and realized it must've been early because there wasn't anyone bustling about below her. Leaning on the balcony's stone railing, she looked below it to where the large pool lay. The still waters cast in shadows of the trees in the night, were dark and reflective, not yet warmed by the morning sun. She immediately thought of those eyes, the eyes of the King, the eyes of her King, her husband.

There was a short knock at her door, but she really didn't feel ready to start her day. Memories and emotions swirled in her head, and she wanted to retreat into herself. The relentless early bird rapped at the door again. Liana sighed as she heard her door swing open with a bang and wondered what all the fuss was about. She poked her head through the drapes to see Nicolai stood short of breath and looked around her room. Rolling her eyes at his dramatic entrance, she pulled her head back out of the drapes and held them shut in front of her face.

"You okay?" he asked with worry in his voice.

He was on the other side of the curtains and longed to rip them open but didn't want to upset her.

"I'm fine. What's wrong with you? Why are you up here so early?" she asked shortly.

"Come on, have some breakfast; we need to meet with the others," he said quickly and extended his hand through the curtain.

"Ehhh…" She moved around his outstretched hand, flung the curtains open and crossed the room to sit on the edge of the bed while she mumbled, "I don't really feel up to anything today."

"Well, I'm not going to be the last one up here after you," he said while he tried to reason with her, but after a moment, his face lit up. "Come on; I have an idea."

He walked out of the room. She looked to Striker, who was fast asleep in her bed and quietly made her way out of the room, curious to see what Nicolai was up to. As she followed closely behind him, they made their way quietly down the hallway. He put his hand out and asked for her to be quiet as they neared the balcony over the foyer. Voices sounded from downstairs in the kitchen; they laughed and carried on as they ate.

No one was usually up this early, but today was different for some reason. Nicolai motioned her forward, and they crept down the stairs silently. The two of them slipped around the wall at the end of the stairs into the open ballroom. Liana followed Nicolai across the large open room toward a back hallway that led to a back door. Before she knew it, the two of them ran across the side field that led to the forest's edge.

"Where are we going?" she asked.

"You'll see."

He led her through the trees to a small clearing that overlooked a valley full of beautiful blossoming trees and wildflowers. He sat on the grass and opened a pack that he carried. Liana sat beside him and wondered for a second when he picked it up, but soon could care less as she noticed the pack contained breakfast. She smiled at him because she had worked up quite an appetite. He pulled out a blueberry muffin, handed it to her, and caught her smile.

"What?" he asked and couldn't help but smile back at her.

She looked down at the muffin and shook her head with her reply, "You just know me."

"Well, I've known you longer than you have… If that makes sense."

"Whatever you say," she said before she looked up at him and laughed.

He laughed with her as they enjoyed a light breakfast.

"I miss this," he said while his gaze drifted off to look out into the distance. "You know, we used to be like this all the time, sneaking off, no worries." He smiled, and looked down at the ground while he continued, "We'd always come up with excuses to try to get each other out of training." The smile faded from his face, and his head dropped slightly before he mumbled, "Then they took you to be Queen… everything changed after that."

Liana studied his face as he reflected on his memories.

After a moment of silence, she spoke softly, "I just wish I could remember."

He shook his head, while he looked at her and replied, "Enjoy it while you can, some memories aren't as pleasant to relive."

Liana let the silence linger for a moment as she looked out into the distance before she asked, "You mean like when they banished me?"

She glanced sideways and searched for his reaction.

"I figured it was only a matter of time before the memories started to trickle back," he began slowly, "but they had no right to do that to you!"

His voice escalated as he stood and turned from her.

"It's over though, what can you do about it at this point?" she asked while she got to her feet.

"Well…"

"Well, what? Are you going to kill them or something?"

Her voice escalated and cut the air in a harsh tone that felt unlike her. He turned and stared at her for a moment, anger on his face.

"Come on, we need to get back," he said while he moved around her and bumped into her shoulder as he walked off without even a glance back.

When she struggled to keep pace with him, she yelled out, frustrated, "Nic, slow down!"

He stopped in his tracks, head bent toward the ground. Her pace slowed in response and allowed her to catch her breath. Before long, she was able to catch up to Nicolai. An eerie silence fell across the trees, and she suddenly noticed he didn't walk with her.

Liana turned abruptly and saw Nicolai in the same place he had stopped before. Only now, he was crouched and examined the ground. Something brushed across Liana's leg, and instantly caused her to jump to the side of the path. She caught her breath as she looked down to see the panting smile of Striker that beamed back at her.

Confusion filled her voice as she muttered toward Striker, "When did yo-?"

They jerked their heads up in unison as the sounds of barking resonated in the distance. Instantly, Nicolai broke out in a sprint and grabbed Liana's wrist as he passed her. The barking grew louder as they approached the house. In a short time, a white furry blur of what Liana assumed was Zhati cut across their path and headed in the direction they had come from. Nicolai pressed onward toward the house and practically dragged Liana.

"Wait, what's going on?" she asked in between breaths. "Shouldn't we see where he's going?"

He didn't look back at her, only gave her a dismissive, "No."

Liana grew very impatient while she glared at the back of Nicolai's head. It always seemed she could never get any real communication out of him. Channeling her frustration, she closed her eyes and searched for Nicolai's thoughts.

*Past our barriers, t*he distant voice of Nicolai echoed in and out as if they were in a large, cavernous structure, distant from each other, *know the way...*

Her eyes opened suddenly when she realized they had reached the house. He released her wrist and put a hand on her back while he guided her into the house. As they entered the kitchen, Arietta ran out to meet them. The room swirled slightly as dizziness set in on Liana.

"Oh, thank God! Liana!" Arietta shouted as she embraced her, then immediately took a step back and eyed her for a split second before she turned her attention to Nicolai. She hurriedly said, "I think someon-"

Nicolai raised a hand up to silence her while he added, "I know."

She walked toward the main hall with Nicolai while she said, "Khius went with the do-"

"Get the others together quickly."

Arietta glared at Nicolai with a frustration laced face but closed her mouth tightly and turned from him to run up the stairs.

"Come on," he said impatiently over his shoulder to Liana as he walked to a door near the bottom of the stairs.

Silently, she followed behind him through the door, into a small basement room with a bunch of chairs and cabinets. She made her way to the back of the room where she leaned against the wall, arms crossed over her chest, and watched Nicolai as he paced with his head down, consumed in his thoughts. It wasn't long before the room was filled with the other members of the house. They all sat quietly until Arietta returned. As she closed the door, an out of breath Khius squeezed in.

"Well?" Nicolai asked while he looked up impatiently at Khius.

Khius stood at the front of the room with Nicolai as Arietta moved to Liana in the back. He hunched over to catch his breath as an annoyed Nicolai crossed his arms over his chest.

"I didn't… see anyone," Khius finally said in between breaths.

"What?" Nicolai asked angrily through his teeth while he looked at Khius in disbelief.

"I didn't," Khius said as he threw his arms out dramatically. "I did a perimeter sweep. I saw some tracks, but they disappeared after a short distance. The wolves are already back."

Nicolai looked at Khius while he moved to sit in one of the chairs. He glanced briefly at Arietta, who nodded, then he spoke to the whole room.

"We need to tighten our watch over the next few days and plan to move out. Our location has been comprised. Wes," Nicolai said as he looked to Wes, who had his chin in his hand, propped up on his elbow on his leg. "Can you set up another barrier and try to find somewhere temporary we can go?"

Wes nodded to Nicolai, stood, and disappeared with a popping noise. Liana's mouth dropped as she stared at the spot he stood just a moment before. No one seemed the least bit alarmed at what she had just witnessed. She swallowed slowly, leaned back against the wall, and now examined each person as Nicolai rambled on to each of them. One by one, they stood and left the room. Liana began to lose interest, unsure of what took place. She thought back to what she had heard when she tried to listen to Nicolai.

*What did he mean,* she thought to herself, *past our barriers? What was past our barriers?*

She began to grow nervous at the idea of whatever or whoever had everyone on high alert.

Arietta tapped her arm and spoke softly, "Let's go."

She nodded to the door. Liana pushed off the wall, moved around the now empty chairs, and followed behind Arietta.

Nicolai grabbed her arm as she was about to walk through the doorway, and asked in a hushed tone, "A moment?"

She nodded and stepped back into the room. His hand moved to the door to close it and remained there as he spoke to keep it closed.

"Watch who's head you're trying to get into," he said sternly.

"I… what are you talking about."

He let out a short, irritated sigh and rolled his eyes with his reply, "I can hear your thoughts when you listen to mine."

Without giving her a chance to respond, he jerked open the door and stormed off. She stood there for a moment, embarrassed that he knew she had pried into his head and wondered what sort of thoughts he may have heard from her.

Arietta poked her head back in the door before she asked, "You good?"

Liana cleared her throat.

"Yea," she said quickly before she walked out of the room.

Arietta led her immediately up the stairs and stopped at her room.

She coughed awkwardly as she turned to face Liana and quietly said, "So…"

"Uh... What's this?" Liana asked hostilely.

"Just sit tight for a little, okay?" Arietta reasoned while she took a step toward Liana, who backed away.

"So, what? I'm grounded?"

"Liana, it's not… safe right now. Just… stay put for a little. If you need to go anywhere, just bring someone with you. I'll be back to check on you in a few."

Arietta moved around Liana slowly and attempted to gently nudge her toward her room.

"You've got to be kidding," she responded quietly as her head dropped.

"Temporary… please?" Arietta pleaded with her quietly in her ear and placed her hands on Liana's shoulders.

Without saying a word, Liana shrugged Arietta's hands off and went into her room before she slammed the door behind her.

○ ○ ○

Liana paced about her room while she worked up the courage to talk to Nicolai. The previous day raced around in her mind and threatened to drive her crazy. She took a deep breath and stormed out of her room toward his. As she turned to knock on his door, she noticed it was slightly ajar.

After Liana cleared her throat, she called out, "Uhh, Nicolai?"

She waited a moment but heard nothing and thought it was strange that he left his door open. Using her foot, she gently nudged the door open a bit more and peered in. When she didn't see him in the room, Liana turned to leave. As she did, something on his dresser caught her eye. She pushed open his door the rest of the way and walked in. As she got closer, she noticed it was the small, grey book she had stashed previously. Liana stopped in her tracks, confused.

*How would he have that,* she asked herself.

Quickly, she backed out of his room and shut the door. As she turned to walk back to her room, she bumped into Khius.

"Woah there!" he exclaimed while he laughed, and he backed away from her. "Hey, you okay?" he said in a more serious tone as he caught sight of her disgruntled demeanor.

"Hey, Khius! I'm great! Want to go for a jog?" she asked loudly, with an oddly cheerful tone as she raised her eyebrows at him and leaned her head toward him.

"No, not really…. Are you sure you're okay?" he asked, puzzled.

Liana sighed and rolled her eyes as she threw up her hands in disbelief. Khius' mouth fell open in a dumbfounded fashion before he caught on to what she implied.

"On second thought, that sounds great!" he said and suddenly matched her volume as he looked around.

Liana wasted no time; as their feet hit the pavement of the path that looped the house, she started in on Khius, "Would've been nice to know that my mind-reading abilities are a two-way street!"

"What? What are you talking about?" Khius asked and looked around them before he rested his attention on Liana.

She grabbed Khius' wrist, and jerked his arm backward to get him to turn to her.

*You know exactly,* she screamed at him in her thoughts, *what I'm talking about!*

Khius let out a snort and short chuckle before he replied, "Okay, I should've told you."

"You think?" she asked, annoyed as she released his wrist from her grip. "Would've been much easier to hear coming from you instead of *Nicolai.*"

"Oh…" he said awkwardly as he rubbed the back of his neck, "yea, I can't imagine that was pleasant. Sorry."

"Anyway, what's going on?" she asked and tried to shift the topic to the more crucial issue at hand as she took off into a jog again.

Khius looked around cautiously and ran to catch up to her before he spoke in a quiet tone, "Casimir is trying to break through to take you."

"Why? Why won't Nicolai tell me anything?" she asked while she matched the volume of his voice.

"He doesn't want you to freak out."

She rolled her eyes, irritated.

"Aren't I The Queen?" she asked while her hands flung in the air as she said her title with a sarcastic, mocking tone.

Khius laughed.

"You are, and Nicolai hated when you became The Queen," he said as he matched her tone.

"Regardless, shouldn't I get a say or at least get to *know* what's going on?"

"Ehh…" He looked around cautiously again before he replied, "Probably not if it compromises your safety."

She opened her mouth as if to rebuttal but decided against it. Instead, she changed the subject again.

"Whatever. I have to get out of here. I'm like a prisoner. I feel like a sitting duck."

"Yes!" Khius said as though he won an argument. "That's what I've been trying to tell him!"

Liana stopped and bent over with her hands on her knees while she tried to catch her breath.

Quietly and in between breaths, she asked, "So what's the plan."

He matched her posture, his head near hers, and whispered, "Tomorrow morning, be ready."

# Chapter 14
## *In the Shadows*

Liana climbed the length of stairs to her room, and desperately gripped the wooden banister for balance as her muscles protested any further labor. She stopped to pat the large head of Zhati, who sat guard at her door before she made her way to the shower. Liana dropped her garments on the floor along her way before she entered the large, tiled shower room. The silver knobs on the shower wall creaked as she turned them.

Slowly, she leaned against the corner of the shower as the hot liquid flowed over her skin. The collective pain in her muscles melted away as steam filled the room. After a moment lost in thought, she washed quickly, for the soft, warm bed that stood beyond the bathroom doors called out to her. As she rinsed the foam from her hair, she heard a clatter from the other side of the bathroom door. When she stepped from the water, she reached for a towel, and dried her face as she moved toward the door.

Her hand rested on the door for only a moment before she pushed it open, and revealed a massive room beyond her, very much unlike the place she had spent many nights in recently. Through narrowed eyes, she suspiciously looked behind her to find a smaller, brighter room with mirrors, clouded by the steam, instead of her shower room. Her heart pounded as she turned back toward the large open room and entered it slowly.

"Just a dream… just a dream," she repeated to herself as she took slow breaths and tried to calm down.

Something felt different about this one. With another breath, she continued forward as the dread inside her rose. In the middle of the room stood a silver bed with flowing, sheer, white curtains that fell from the vaulted ceiling and stretched to the floor far from the bed they surrounded. Shielded by the curtains, on the far side of the bed, she could hear a commotion.

The deafening pounding of her heart in her ears was soon replaced by her own scream. Grasping her mouth, she pleaded with herself to be silent while she fell to her knees and tears blotted her vision. On the floor, in a pile of robes, lay the man she had given her heart to. His crown lay at his feet in a pool of blood, where a dark figure stood. He quickly concealed a glowing blade that dripped of blood, in his robes. Liana scrambled to her feet as the shadowy, hooded figure moved toward her.

Dripping from the shower, she slipped, and her face collided with the white wooden floor. The dark figure closed in on her quickly and lifted her into his arms. She struggled against him in vain as he fled from the room to an open balcony. From the balcony, Liana could see a massive garden with shrubs, flowering trees, and beautiful vining flowers that stretched out as far as she could see. As they reached a wall, Liana looked back through the garden to see a large castle. Guards shouted from all directions while their armored boots marched heavily as they pursued her.

The air suddenly grew dark and stale around them. Liana was able to free herself from his grasp long enough to deal a sharp blow to his stomach. Instantly, the man released his grip on her and let her fall to the solid ground. She rose to her feet, quickly turned from the man, and ran in the direction away from him. The territory was unfamiliar, and she could no longer hear the sounds from the Kingdom. Panic began to set in as she was barely able to see anything about her. She repeatedly tripped over jagged rocks and jutted roots. She paused for only a moment and tried to catch her breath.

"Why do you run from me?" he whispered in her ear.

She drew a sharp breath inwardly and moved to run again, but he caught her arm. Reaching around quickly, she punched at his shrouded face and kicked at his legs, but her blows went right through him as though he were a shadow.

"Stop!" he yelled angrily.

"What have you done?" she motioned behind her in the direction she thought the castle lay. "Why would you...?"

Tears streamed down her face and cut off her words at the realization of her King's life being taken. Her chest began to tighten, and her breathing became uneven as everything around her spun.

"I did it for you," he said quietly as he lifted her in his arms and made his way through the strange dark forest.

She wept into his chest as the twisted scene faded into that of a shadowy kingdom. The buildings stood tall, dark, and twisted. They seemed to lean in toward her as she passed by. The man carried Liana into the courtyard of the dark castle that towered over the village. A group of men took her from him and drug her away. They carried her down a long hallway lit by candlelight. As they reached the end of the hall, they threw open large doors that led to a dark room. Liana felt their rough hands on her back as they shoved her into the room and slammed the doors in her face.

She was immediately overtaken by a group of women. They stripped her of her now filthy and ripped bath towel, bathed her, and quickly dressed her in a midnight blue, flowing velvet gown that was embellished with tiny silver beads. They steered her toward a large bed that lay in the center of the room and sat her gently on its edge. The harsh, frigid atmosphere of the room began to overtake her, and she shivered. The rigid bed was draped in flowing black covers the reached the floor. The dark wooden frame was stained blue with strange engravings scattered across it.

Shortly after the woman left the room, the doors flung open with a man that stood in their frame. He walked slowly toward Liana. She got to her feet and retreated behind the bed from the man who had brought her there. Before she couldn't make out his face, but suddenly she could clearly see that she knew him. The dark hair that hung messily around his dark eyes, that intrusive grin, was all too familiar. Casimir reached for her and tucked her hair behind her ear.

"Now, we can finally be together."

His voice was distant and echoed as she tried to focus. A crash sounded, and light flooded the room. Suddenly, she felt water pulsing on her face and looked around to find she was back in her shower.

Yelling sounded from her bedroom, "Liana!"

She sat up from the corner of the shower that she had curled against as Nicolai rushed into the bathroom. Striker followed closely behind him, and ran out behind Nicolai to greet Liana. Nicolai grabbed a towel off the wall as he made his way to her.

"Liana, come on, get up," Nicolai said while he stooped next to her and reached up to turn off the water.

Its icy talons had chilled Liana to the bone. She didn't know if she shook from the freezing water or the grip of the nightmare. Nicolai led her into her room where others bustled about. Some locked doors and windows, while others paced and checked every corner of Liana's room. She took no notice of the others while her eyes remained unblinkingly fixed on the floor. She sat stiffly on her bed, fixated on her King that had come to pass, by the hands of the very being that she invited into her life which set her destiny in motion.

A pain stretched across her chest; she hoped it was death. It was as if she was being bound with barbed wire. Her chest grew tighter with each painful breath, and as the pain intensified, her breathing became shallow and uneven. Striker licked at her hand and arm as he tried to bring her any comfort he could. It was then she noticed Nicolai stood before her with a hooded sweatshirt and pants held out. When she didn't take them, he took a closer look at her expression and became worried.

"Liana," his voice echoed in the distance, "Liana, I need you to pull it together, just for a little bit. Please."

He held her face in his hands; she tried to focus on his eyes and gradually comfort washed over her. He looked so composed. Liana couldn't pull her mind off what she had seen. She tried to focus as she looked down at herself. Suddenly very aware of her post-shower state, she gripped the towel to her body and looked back up at Nicolai.

"Liana, I'm so sorry," Nicolai said as a look of remorse passed over his face.

"What's going on?" she asked, bewildered as she began to realize there were other people in her room.

"We must get you to safety. She's leaving now, and *we* must go. Quickly," he said while he urged her to move.

Liana realized Nicolai referred to the others that escorted Arietta in place of Liana as a decoy while she escaped. As if on cue, gunfire broke through the wooden panels that were drawn over the window. Liana was instantly under a dogpile and pushed to the floor. Gasping for air, she pulled herself out from under several bodies and hurriedly pulled on a pair of sweatpants and a hooded sweatshirt.

"They've broken through our line of defenses," Khius said in a hushed tone to the others as he stood, and blocked Liana, who scrambled to clothe herself.

Without notice, Khius yanked Liana to the ground and pulled himself over the top of her as another round of gunfire sprayed the room from outside. Wes crouched down next to Liana and the others, weapon in hand, a look of confusion on his face.

"That doesn't make sense," Wes said toward Nicolai. "How did they make it through so fast? It's as if they…"

"We've got to go now," Khius interrupted forcefully as he guided Liana toward her closet, where a trap door lay behind an old trunk in the back.

Khius shoved a pair of night vision goggles into Liana's chest then motioned for her to wait in the corner of the closet while some of the others started filing through the hatch. Liana slipped the goggles on and let them rest on her forehead while she waited. Her fingers brushed against the coarse fur of Striker's, and she realized they couldn't take him this way. She bent down and placed her forehead against his. Striker let out a soft whine in response as if he knew already.

"Don't worry, boy, meet us out there," she whispered as she ruffled his ears.

Striker let out a low grumble before he licked her hand and ran out of the room. Once almost everyone was through, Khius motioned for her.

"After you," he said with hand outstretched and charming smile.

She took his hand as she lowered herself into the hatch and grasped the ladder. Liana's sweaty, shaky hands gripped the cold metal rungs of the ladder as she descended into the darkness. Screams and gunfire sounded from every direction. Her feet hit the ground of the passageway as Khius closed the hatch above, and darkness engulfed the group.

Liana stepped away from the ladder as she slid the goggles over her eyes and clicked them on. She looked around at the tightly linked group of her elite soldiers as they formed a barrier around her. Once Khius joined them, they began to make their way through the halls hidden in the walls of the house. Liana's safety had been compromised; the defenses had been breached, and they needed to get her out to somewhere safer. Several rounds of gunfire sounded exceptionally close to the group, and caused Nicolai to pick up the pace. Nicolai stepped into a small intersection of the passageways and was immediately met by a group of hostiles.

Instantly, the others jumped in response, and aided Nicolai with subduing the group. They struggled against the intruders in a tangle of fists and faces as several rounds of gunfire were discharged in every direction. Khius and Wes stood around Liana in an attempt to shield her and move her away from the struggle. Just as Nicolai and his group overcome the assault from the front, another group approached from the back.

Khius shoved Liana forward into Wes's arms and smacked him on the shoulder. Wes immediately grabbed Liana's shoulders and turned her in Nicolai's direction while he attempted to maneuver her through the flying fists and over the mess of legs from subdued intruders. As they rounded a corner, someone lunged at Wes. They knocked him into Liana, who fell against the wall and to the ground.

In the commotion, Liana's goggles were knocked from her face and kicked out of her reach. She looked around in vain while only darkness met her gaze and began to feel for the wall. The noise of the commotion heightened and pressed in on her in her now sightless state.

"Come on," Khius whispered in her ear as she felt him seize her arm and yank her to her feet.

He raised her hand to his shoulder and began to navigate the twists and turns of the maze. The further they went, the quieter it grew until silence pressed in on them. They paused for a moment, and a grateful Liana leaned against the wall to catch her breath.

"Khi-" her voice was cut off by a finger to her lip that silenced her.

She jerked her head away from the finger, annoyed, and ready to be out of this suffocating situation. After a few seconds, the sound of boots on the wooden floor approached, and Liana felt a hand on her collarbone that pressed her against the wall in response. She held her breath in silence as the air moved by her and indicated the boot-wearing individual's movement. As the sound began to dissipate, she reached up with her hand into the hall. Liana quickly jerked her hand back as she felt the breeze of another individual pass by silently.

After another few seconds, she felt someone nudge her to move, and she happily complied. Before long, Liana could see a small amount of light down the hall. They had finally reached the hatch near the edge of the forest. The hatch stood slightly open. Enough light crept through that Liana could see Nicolai stood at it and listening cautiously. Once he saw the rest of the group arrive, he opened the solid door and poked his head out.

Liana took long, calculated breaths as the walls began to close in on her. She could hear distant yelling and gunfire but tried to focus on anything else. Everyone seemed to press tightly in on her which caused the creeping grip of anxiety to claw at her. After what seemed like an eternity, they signaled to Liana that the coast was clear for her to come out. She ducked through the small stone exit into the high grass of the fields. Khius shut the door behind her and closed the hole in the group that surrounded her.

"We have only a short distance to the forests. Liana will be safer there, but we will have to make our way to the cove," Nicolai said in a hushed tone to the others.

"The cove? What are you going to do? She isn't ready to go back yet. We don't even have the blade," Khius whispered back heatedly.

"She has enough power in her to get through the gate; we'll worry about the rest later. Come on," he said in Khius' direction. "It's the last place they'd look for her."

Khius shot Liana a quick look, and her worries began to grow. Nicolai was trying to take her back to the Kingdom before they even had a chance for *their* plan. She wasn't sure what to do now and wanted desperately to grab Khius and just run for it.

Shouting and gunfire sounded again, several yards from them, but this time it came from outside the house. They all turned their backs on Liana, forming a tight huddle and moved swiftly across the field. Liana ducked low as she followed the group. She looked between Antonio and Nicolai and could see that the edge of the forest was close. The evening light filtered through the trees and made deceptive shadows as an eerie fog began to rise from the ground. Liana grabbed the back of Nicolai's shirt, now not so sure about entering the forest. He turned, slightly annoyed, and looked at her enquiringly.

"Wai-"

Gunfire cut off Liana's words. Khius shoved her to the ground as blood splattered across her face. Someone had been hit, but she couldn't see who. Khius pulled Liana to her feet and pulled her a short distance before she took off to run with the others. Gunfire erupted again right behind them, but every time she turned to see what was going on, Khius shoved her forward. They reached a dense area and started the climb toward a path that would lead to the cove. Their pace began to slow as the noise died down.

"Wait!" Liana panted as she stumbled into Khius' arms.

She frantically wiped the blood from her face. The group stood for a moment and stared at her as she caught her breath.

"Shouldn't we-" Liana stopped mid-sentence when something rustled in the trees behind her.

She turned to face whatever made the noise while Khius moved in front of her and pushed an outstretched arm to move Liana behind him. The group circled around

Liana, ready to strike as a blur of white fur leaped through the trees and uprooted several in the process.

"Zhati!" Liana shouted with relief.

The massive wolf knocked right into the solid chest of Khius which sent him to the ground in a tangle of fur and legs, right at Liana's feet.

"Move!" Khius laughed while he desperately tried to pull the enthusiastic Zhati off him.

A low rumble sounded from the trees where Zhati had leaped out. Purge slowly emerged from the shadows of the tree canopy and knocked Zhati with her head. Zhati stepped back, and allowed Khius to get to his feet before he soaked him in drool with an enthusiastic lick up the side of Khius' face.

"Missed you too," Khius groaned while he wiped globs of sticky drool from his neck and chin.

Relief washed over Liana at the sight of the two wolves. Though they were covered in a mixture of blood, mud, and debris, they were intact. Looking around to the others, she tried to determine who was still with her until a blur of fur rushed at her.

"Striker!" she cried out in relief as she bent to embrace him.

"Great timing. Let's get moving," Nicolai said as he looked around impatiently.

The group formed again around Liana as they moved through the tree line. They moved in unison through the tall, thin trees that were lined with narrow leaves and scattered sparsely across the high grassy area. Zhati perched at the top of a hill and sniffed the air while he waited on the others to reach him. They climbed the small hill quickly and came into an open clearing. Zhati dropped his head as his ears went back, and he let out a low growl.

The two wolves circled Liana's group before they took position on either side of them. Zhati let out a soft howl and began to emit small sparks of electricity. He grew larger, and his white fur sparked with blue volts. In a matter of seconds, the shield of blue and white electrical sparks formed around the group.

"Let's go!" Nicolai said suddenly.

The group moved in unison while they ran under the shield of Zhati through the clearing. Liana looked around as they began to run. As the sun continued to drop, the shadows crept across the clearing.

"Khius!" she shouted as she reached for his arm.

The group halted abruptly in unison as several shadowy figures emerged from the now darkened forest that surrounded the clearing. Liana's heart pounded in her chest as she surveyed the scene. They were quickly surrounded in the middle of the clearing. Countless individuals stepped from the shadows as though they were being birthed by them. Their clothing clung to them in dark, twisted wraps, faces concealed by black coverings, only their piercing, glowing, amber eyes were visible in the dimming light.

Liana's group held their ground, frozen as solid as stone statues. The wolves on either side of the group crouched defensively as a low growl began in Purge. Liana looked to Purge to see that her sight was fixed in the distance. She followed her gaze to a figure that walked in the shadows. After a moment of trying to focus on the figure, Liana realized her eyes were fixed on Casimir. He now casually strolled in their direction, the usual smug grin on his face.

Without warning, Purge lifted her head and let out a long piercing howl. The ground shook beneath Liana as Purge's howl gained power. Liana looked up to see the shrouded figures that surrounded them had been knocked off their feet. Even Casimir staggered at the force of the howl; he dropped to a knee briefly before he stood and brushed himself off. He looked up at Liana as irritation spread on his face.

"Liana," he called out from across the field, eyes fixed on her as he walked toward her and taunted, "it doesn't have to be like this."

Liana gripped Khius' arm nervously as Casimir edged closer, but their group said nothing.

"Fine," Casimir said halfheartedly before he glanced behind her.

Liana followed his glance over her shoulder.

"Zhati!" she called out in horror while she reached for the unsuspecting wolf.

Behind him, a small shadowy blur of an individual arose from the tall grass with a long, dark shadowy blade in hand. The person leaped at the shield; as the figure's feet connected with the electrical field, they kicked off it and jumped directly over Zhati. The unsuspecting wolf lifted his head as the being soared over. In one quick motion, the figure landed next to Zhati and hauled the shadowy blade through his flesh. As the individual's feet hit the ground, so did Zhati. The electrical field slowly dissipated as Zhati's blood spilled across the dirt.

"No!" Khius yelled out furiously.

Tears streamed down Liana's face, over her hand that clasped her open mouth. She quickly looked back at Casimir, who seemed quite pleased with himself. He raised his hand, and discharged the handgun in it, in

Liana's direction. Khius yanked her from the group as a round connected with his shoulder.

"Khius!" Liana called out, concerned.

"There's no time! Run!" he shouted frantically as he looked over Liana's shoulder at Purge.

They pushed their way through the others who fought off the countless soldiers that made up the shadowy army of Casimir's. As the last of the electrical field fed into Purge's body, she let out a massive, ear-splitting howl and began to grow. Everyone near her dropped to their knees while they held their heads in agony. The impact of her cry shifted the ground and broke free large pieces of land that the others leaped over as they fought off the swarming shadowy figures.

Several figures swarmed Purge and after only a moment, dropped her to the ground. After only seconds, she grew four times her original size. In the distance, Khius and Liana disappeared into the dark trees while Purge and the others fought back their attackers. Casimir stood back while he took the scene in with a look of frustration that settled on his face as he realized Liana was nowhere to be seen.

He moved around the edge of the commotion in search of her. As he reached the edge of the clearing, a massive force knocked him from his feet and against a tree. Casimir lay toppled over on the ground at its base. Purge rested her massive paw on his chest and pinned him to the ground. She growled while blood dripped from her open jaw onto Casimir's cheek. Casimir moved his head just in time as she snapped at him and grazed his cheek with her sharp teeth. Casimir yelled out, frustrated as he struggled to free himself from under Purge's weight.

"I don't have time for this nonsense!" he shouted as he pulled his head back slightly and collided it with Purge's.

She yelped and shook her head as she staggered to the side just enough to free Casimir from her crushing weight. He rolled over and scrambled to his feet as she snapped at him. Just as she lunged in his direction, a solid shadowy form collided with her side and sent her back a few feet. Casimir brushed himself off and, with a smile, disappeared.

# Chapter 15
## *Forgive Me*

"Please," Liana breathed heavily behind Khius. "I need… to stop," she said in between breaths as she slowed to a walk.

Khius didn't argue. The trees around them were quiet now that they had put some ground between themselves and the attack. She could hear crickets chirp and the occasional hoot of an owl in the distance as if the rest of their surroundings were completely unaware of what took place not far away. The light around them diminished quickly, especially in the increasing density of the tree cover. Khius took a few deep breaths as he turned in a circle and examined the area while he waited for Liana.

"Okay," she said softly as she walked up next to him, "let's keep moving."

"Wait."

He put an arm up and stopped Liana in her tracks. The air around them had grown eerily quiet now, not even the crickets dared to perform. Liana held her breath, sure to not move even a muscle. Khius looked at Liana and jerked his head in the direction they faced while he signaled for them to move on. Just as he took a step forward, he was met with the solid dark form of Purge. Her size had returned to normal, and she was battle-worn. Her fur dripped with blood and was caked with patches of grass and dirt.

"Purge," Khius cried out in relief as he dropped to his knees in front of her.

She sat and lowered her head to his, resting, so they were eye to eye.

"I am so sorry," Khius said in between sobs, "I never meant for-"

His words were cut off as Purge leaned against him and rested her head on his back in a sort of embrace. She stood after a moment, licked his tears, and let out a soft bark. He nodded to her, and she took off into the trees. Khius remained on his knees; head bowed as the sounds of her paws as they hit the ground were swallowed up by the dense vegetation. Branches suddenly broke nearby. Liana and Khius looked up in unison as Nicolai tumbled out of a mess of bushes.

"There you are! Thank God! Come on," he said as he moved past Khius, "we need to go now."

Nicolai moved ahead of them into the trees and didn't wait for Khius to get to his feet. Liana approached Khius cautiously and rested a hand on his shoulder. She gave it a small squeeze to offer him some sort of sympathy for his loss before she followed behind Nicolai. Striker sat next to Khius for a moment and let out a soft whimper.

"I know," Khius said in response to Striker as he got to his feet.

Striker nudged Khius' hand with his nose before he trotted off to Liana's side. They straggled passively behind Nicolai. Exhaustion and the stillness of the trees about them had weakened their sense of urgency.

Nicolai turned in an irritated tone and said, "We *must* keep moving."

"You don't think we know that?" Khius said shortly, annoyance heavy in his tone.

"I'm just trying to keep Liana safe," he shot back at Khius harshly.

"You're trying to *save* her, not keep her safe," Khius spat as he now came face to face with Nicolai.

Sensing the tension between the two and fearing their noise would attract unwelcome attention, Liana pushed between them.

"Let's go," she said tiredly, without looking at them.

"What are you trying to say?" Nicolai's voice continued, though the crunching of twigs indicated to Liana that they at least moved.

"You aren't even thinking of her safety. Just busy trying to be the *one* that saves her."

"You really have the nerve t-" Nicolai's raised voice was harshly interrupted by a fist to the face.

At hearing the commotion, Liana turned but was immediately met with Khius. He threw her to the ground and stood over her as a group of soldier-like aggressors swarmed him. Liana instantly regretted not maximizing her time with Antonio while she had the opportunity. Now she lay helpless as the others fought to defend her. Khius was slowly losing the battle, and Nicolai lay incoherent amongst the roots of a huge tree only a short distance away. Through Khius' legs, Liana saw someone emerge from the distant trees and make their way toward Nicolai while he stirred.

*Liana run,* Nicolai mouthed as the figure closed in on him.

The shadowy form pressed the heel of its heavy, black boot into Nicolai's neck and pinned him amongst the tangled roots of the tree. Pale fingers of the attacker gripped a small pistol and yanked it from a holster on his leg before they rested the firearm between Nicolai's eyes and pressed it to his skin. Liana reached for Nicolai desperately.

"Nicolai!" she cried out in unison with the deafening release of the firearm which caused the shadowy figure's attention to turn toward her.

"No!" a scream of pain and despair emanated from the depths of Liana, accompanied by blue and silver electrical currents that moved like a shockwave through the trees.

The force knocked Khius, accompanied by his several attackers and Nicolai's executioner, yards away from her. They fell flat on their backs and remained motionless. Gasping for air and gripping her chest, she collapsed backward on the forest floor. Liana laid still while she stared at the trees as they swayed in and out of focus in the canopy above her. The darkness closed in around her, and she could feel herself slipping away. The sudden shock of a cold, wet nose to her neck widened Liana's eyes in an instant. She slowly rolled to her side and lifted herself to sit.

"Striker!" she cried out in a stifled whisper as her eyes fell not only on her beloved companion but the motionless bodies around her.

Her legs shook uncontrollably as she attempted to stand. Still weakened by the use of her powers, she crawled along the ground toward Nicolai. Once she reached his feet, she sat there and stared at Nicolai's unmoving body in disbelief. Tears streamed from her unblinking eyes down her pale cheeks. Unable to move, she remained at his side; deaf to her surroundings and unable to think while her gaze remained fixed on his form.

Striker began to pace back and forth next to her while he let out soft whimpers. Liana felt the jolt of his cold nose on her cheek and snapped her out of her current grieving state. She looked around as the others began to stir and knew she couldn't remain there any longer. Gripping onto Striker, she attempted to stand again. This time she was able to get to her feet with little effort. While she drew in a deep breath, she turned to look on Nicolai one last time.

Eyes fixed on Nicolai, she knew she didn't have much time and turned to leave but knocked into something firm. A sigh escaped her lips as she turned to meet the gaze of Casimir that burned down at her. The ever-present cocky grin was spread even wider on his face now. Liana did take a small measure of pleasure from the fact that he was dirt-covered and in a somewhat disheveled state from meeting Purge and her electrical outburst previously.

"Your little friends are all gone now. There's no point in running," he said with a laugh as he gestured to Nicolai, an almost proud look on his face.

"I'm not going to run," she said, though her voice didn't feel her own.

Barely audible and devoid of emotion, she stared at him, a blank expression on her face. Casimir half laughed, though her previous statement was enough to steal his smile.

"Finally recognized your fate?" he asked as he stepped closer to her.

She backed into a tree behind her and braced against it for support. He moved in uncomfortably close to her while a sadistic grin spread across his face. Liana looked past Casimir to the limp form of Nicolai on the ground as the others around her stirred more.

In a hushed voice, she simply said, "Just take me."

"Come on! Let's go," Casimir said shortly to the others, almost annoyed at Liana for not engaging in his banter.

He grabbed Liana by the arm and immediately jumped back as a loud, zapping sound emitted from her.

"What the-" he looked down at a growling Striker.

Liana realized as quickly as Casimir what happened, and she shoved him before she turned to run. A cold, short laugh followed by the sound of a firearm reverberated behind Liana. She stopped in her steps, unable to turn around and confirm what her imagination vividly painted. Casimir wrapped his cold talons around Liana's bicep.

Once his skin made contact with hers without resistance, he harshly steered her away from the others. She looked back before the scene could be swallowed up behind her to see a lifeless Striker that rest soundly at the base of a tree. Though it felt like a rock was lodged in her throat, and tears fought for the chance to rain down, her expression remained flat and lifeless. She stared off in the distance and wished she could have just one more morning cuddle with her best friend, one more cold nose to wake her up.

*What did they even die for,* she asked herself.

Here she walked defeated and in the hands of the enemy, while she marched off to who knows what. She knew she had to pull herself together, but all she could see was the panting smile of Striker and the faces of all those who fought in vain to keep her from Casimir. Her jaw tightened in anger, though the rest of her face remained devoid of emotion. Casimir's grip gradually moved to the back of Liana's neck as they walked briskly through the forest.

"I'm glad you decided to see things my way," he said with a grin that seemed to be permanently glued to his face.

Liana kept silent and tried to formulate some sort of plan as they made their way through the dense trees. After what felt like a lifetime to Liana, they reached a small clearing. The tiny, bright opening in the woods was made up of a sandy beach and pond shaded by the shadows of the trees. Across the water roared a waterfall. It would've been beautiful under any other circumstances, but an uneasy feeling grew in Liana.

"Go," Casimir said before he shoved Liana in the water.

"You'd kill to get your hands on me so we can go for a swim?" she asked in a mocking tone while she turned to glare at him.

"I said go," he said in an agitated tone as he rolled his eyes.

He grabbed her shirt and, in one swift motion, turned her and shoved her in the back, which sent her face-first into the water. She pulled herself to her feet and choked out mouthfuls of water.

"Come on; we're running out of time," he said to the others while he looked around at them and waded into the water.

As he caught up with Liana, he began to drag her toward the other side of the water. Once they reached the furthest side, he submerged, and dragged her below with him. They surfaced in a low ceiling cave with a small rock shelf that Casimir pulled himself up on. The others gradually surfaced next to Liana. She stayed partially submerged while she took in the scene around her.

The walls of the cave were a dark cobalt color with strange white symbols scattered across them like stars in the night. A light came from a source on the other side of Casimir that Liana could not see from her position in the water. When she looked around her from one side of the cave to the other, she soon came face to face with Casimir.

"Waiting on you," he said in a quiet but stern voice as he held out his hand.

Apprehensively, she reached for him.

He began to hoist her up to the surface where he sat and whispered, "You won't be sorry," with the same sly grin on his face.

"No, but you will," Liana said as she kicked off the ledge where he sat and yanked with all her force on his hold.

Casimir toppled over her into the water with a loud splash. Liana quickly threw her head back and connected with his before she dove into the water. Liana searched desperately for the way back to the pond they had come from. The water was getting dark around her, and she couldn't tell which direction they had come from.

She felt someone tightly grab ahold of her abdomen. They pulled her back toward the strange cave. With a desperate wiggle while she tried to free herself, she turned and realized she was in the arms of Casimir. Liana pulled at his hands and tried to break his grip. Her elbow repeatedly dug deep into his chest as she attempted to free herself from his hold to no avail.

Her vision became blurry as her need for air became dire. She gave one last thrust with her elbow and drove it into Casimir's face. The crunch of his nose against her elbow gave Liana the hope she was looking for when he quickly released his grip.

Desperate for air, she quickly surfaced. Her lungs gratefully filled with air as she frantically swam for the edge of the cave walls. As she reached the side of the wall and took a deep breath to swim below, several hands overwhelmed her. Painful grasps drug Liana from the water and pinned her against the cold stone floor.

Liana looked on in horror, unable to move under the hands that dug into her skin. As Casimir jerked himself out of the water, he lunged at her and grinded his fist into her face several times before his men pulled him away. A large cut opened above her eyebrow, and she could feel a warm liquid as it ran down her jawline. She sat up slowly on her elbows as the cave spun around her. In seconds Casimir lunged again, grabbed her by the hair and forced her face to the cave floor.

"Hold her, we'll make this quick," he said through his teeth at the others.

She struggled in vain as several hands pinned her to the cold, smooth surface of the cave floor. A sting spread across her body as Casimir cut into the skin of her back. With each draw of his blade, debilitating memories flooded back to Liana. Gradually she stopped resisting as the pain gripped her and spread to every nerve, accompanied by each painful memory as they played slowly in her mind.

Without warning, Casimir stood and admired his work. He tossed the knife into a small pool of water, opposite of where they had come into the cave. The water began to transform into a thicker consistency and appeared to be lit from below. Casimir stooped next to Liana, lifted her head by her hair and kissed her on her forehead.

"See you soon," he whispered before he stood to kick Liana's weak form into the strange pool of liquid.

The water around Liana cradled her in a warm, soft blanket that grew bright and cut off all sound. Blinded, she closed her eyes. Memories raced across her eyelids in distorted fragments. From a distance across a crowd, she saw a young Nicolai and herself sparring, surrounded by a group. Foggy memories flickered by of a bright field that reached to a dark forest. She saw herself in Casimir's arms; Nicolai furious and upset while he lectured her about the boundaries of the Kingdom when he caught her coming back from the edges of the dark forest where Casimir's kingdom lay.

The memories faded into each other as they poured back, and Liana soon saw the King when he picked her to be by his side. Soon after, she saw him being cut down by Casimir. She looked around to find herself on a large, dark bed that lay in the center of a cold and unforgiving room. The doors in front of her flung open while Casimir stood in their frame.

"Now we can finally be together," he said as he embraced her.

Tears welled up in her eyes as she stared up at him.

"At what cost?" she asked with a pained whisper.

His hand slowly found the back of her head and held her to his chest.

"Casimir?" she questioned while she tried to remove herself from his embrace but he only pulled her tighter.

"Forgive me," he whispered into her hair as he rested his cheek on the top of her head.

No sooner had his words left his lips that a crippling pain shot through Liana's spine and spread across every fiber of her body as if she were being dipped into a furnace of white-hot flames. She struggled against Casimir's grip as she screamed out. Seconds felt like centuries as Liana fought against the pain. Casimir finally gave way and stood back while he let her collapse to the floor. As she became accustomed to the fire coursing through her, she looked up. Instantly she recognized the stone handled blade in Casimir's hand that now dripped with her own blood; the very same blade that Casimir had used to slay the King was now clear, drained of its power.

"What have you done?" she screamed in horror as small, blue electrical currents crossed her skin.

The room grew dark as her memory faded into a battlefield surrounded by her troops that faced Casimir's. Liana watched the memory from a distance as she saw herself plead with Casimir to give himself up. She watched as a bright light came between them and overcame the entire battlefield. Memories blurred by quickly of her waking on the battlefield; the scorched ground stretched out for miles, scattered with the lifeless bodies of fallen soldiers.

The horrific scene before her faded to a council of elders in her village. Women and men clad in white, and golden robes sat before her. They held her responsible for the death of the King and the troops. Accusations flew back and forth while they painted a nightmare fueled image of a sadistic Liana that plotted to consume all the people's power.

"She must be stopped!" spat a crowd of angry citizens from behind her that were barely secured by a wall of guards.

"You let him in! You brought this on us!" another yelled before they spat in Liana's direction.

Liana didn't speak. She sat there, on her knees, shackled and surrounded by hateful cries as she stared down at her blood-stained hands, and only saw the faces of those she lost. Crippling devastation gripped her soul. She begged for all this to be over and only longed to be with her King again.

The council declared banishment; to strip her of her powers and send her to another realm. The crowd roared in anger as they called for her head. Tears streamed down Liana's face at the thought of living on. One of the elders lifted a hand to the crowd and silenced them as he slowly rose to his feet.

"Our power lies in the spirit realm here within us. We will perform an ancient ritual removing this traitor's power."

He motioned dismissively to Liana at his feet.

"She will no longer be able to sustain herself in this realm after her power is separated from her. Once she crosses to the human realm, she will not be able to return here without it. No more lives need to be lost on this day. This decision is final."

He looked out over the crowd and though they were still restless they no longer demanded the death of the Queen. He nodded to them with approval. The scene around her grew dark and silent. The water that once surrounded her was gone and the light with it. Liana drew shallow, jagged gasps of air while she lay on the cold dark ground and begged for death. Peace fell over her as she closed her eyes.

○ To Be Continued ○

Cover Art by Ed Espitia; www.edespitia.portfoliobox.io

Made in the USA
Middletown, DE
21 June 2023